Also by Shaina Hawkins

Love is Patient

Breaking Free

One Righteous Person

For more information:
Stephen F. Austin State University Press
P.O. Box 13007 SFA Station
Nacogdoches, Texas 75962
sfapress@sfasu.edu
www.sfasu.edu/sfapress

Book design: Shaina Hawkins
Cover design: Shaina Hawkins
Distributed by Texas A&M Consortium
www.tamupress.com

LIBRARY OF CONGRESS CATALOGING-IN-PUBLICATION DATA
Hawkins, Shaina
One Righteous Person/Shaina Hawkins

ISBN: 978-1-62288-126-0

One Righteous Person

Stories and Poems By

Shaina Hawkins

Stephen F. Austin State University

There is no one righteous, not even one; there is no one who
understands; there is no one who seeks God. All have turned
away, they have together become worthless; there is no one who
does good, not even one.

Romans 3:10-12

Table of Contents

Faith Like a Mustard Seed

"It'll be okay Cecilia", my sister Autumn said to me one evening after dinner as I finished washing up the last of the dishes, "God will take care of it and he won't let anything happen to Claire. You have to trust and have faith."

"I wish I had as much faith as you Autumn, but honestly you don't know what I'm going through right now."

"Don't I? I'm almost positive that you put mom and dad through the same rebellious stage when you were a teenager. You do remember that, don't you?" Autumn asked with a sly smile.

"I remember. But was I ever as bad as Claire at that age?"

"Were you? You really don't remember. Your daughter hasn't even come close to being as bad as you were at that age. I mean if there was an award for the worst daughter of the year it would go to—"

"Okay, I get it. Enough said," I sat down at my small brown circular dining room table and motioned for Autumn to do the same. "I…don't want her to turn out like I did."

"She won't," she said sitting down beside me. "Continue to pray for her and don't be afraid to tell her about the wrong choices you made when you were growing up. You've turned out okay. I mean, it took a while for you to get there, but that might not have happened without the help of your family. Claire will have the help of her mom and dad, plus her favorite aunt, so don't worry, she'll be okay."

"How did you get to have so much faith?"

"I prayed about it every night and asked God to bless me with faith like he gave to the Shunammite woman. Remember her?"

"How could I forget…it was packed into the rest of the early morning devotions that we had when we were kids."

"I miss those mornings," Autumn said with a sigh.

"In a way, so do I."

• • •

"Who was the oldest man that ever lived? Does anyone know?" My mom asked one morning. We first started to do devotions in our household before school every morning when I was seven and my sister was five. I always dreaded morning devotions because I felt that it was a waste of my life. I preferred getting fifteen more minutes in my nice warm bed to doing devotions any day. My sister, being the complete opposite of me, loved it.

"Methuselah," Autumn shouted.

"Correct! And how old was he?"

"Wait…wait…I know this…umm…969?"

"Correct again!"

"Surprise, surprise," I mumbled.

"Okay, now it's time for the story of the day. Has anyone heard the story of the Shunammite woman?" my mother asked.

We shook our heads, "Her story is found in 2 Kings 4:8-37."

"She was known a woman who had great faith regardless of the way the situation looked to others. She never doubted the Lord even in her deepest struggle. This is her story.

There once lived a woman in Shunem who was very wealthy. Her husband farmed the land that they owned and the land produced great crops. They lived in a comfortable home and because of their abundance they were always willing to share with others around them. Her husband made sure that she had the best clothing to wear and provided servants to assist her in all her household duties. The Shunammite and her husband had many servants to work the fields and they always made sure to pay them well for their labor. Her riches, however, were unlike those of her husband. Her riches were not stored on Earth, but in Heaven. God had blessed the Shunammite in every way possible, a loving caring husband who trusted her to carry out the responsibilities of the home, and who loved and respected her.

However, there was one thing that she did not have. She had not been blessed with a child. Over time the Shunammite had learned to be content with the things that God had blessed her with and did not doubt that he would continue to bless her although she was barren. She and her husband continued to grow older and as she was now past the childbearing age, she knew that she would not be able to bear any children. This woman remained content in the fact that God knew what was best and she trusted Him. Why should she question the will of the Lord?

One day a man named Elisha came to Shunem. He was a great prophet in Israel and was traveling through Shumen with his servant, Gehazi. She was outside when she happened to notice the two travelers.

She discussed it with her husband and urged them to stay for a meal. Elisha agreed and he and his servant shared the meal with her that day. Elisha and his servant made such a strong impact on the Shunammite that she invited them to stop by whenever they were in town. They did exactly that. Every time Elisha and Gehazi went to Shunem they would stop by and have meals in her home.

The Shunammite said to her husband, "I am sure that this man who comes here so often is a holy man. Let's build a small room on the roof, put a bed, a table, a chair, and a lamp in it, and he can stay there whenever he visits us." Her husband agreed and soon he and the servants were in the process of building a room for their house guest, Elisha.

One day Elisha returned to Shunem and went to his room to rest. He told Gehazi to call the Shunammite up to his room. When she had approached his room Elisha said to Gehazi, "Ask her what I can do for her in return for all the trouble she has had in providing for our needs. Maybe she would like me to go to the king or the army commander and put in a good word for her."

But she simply replied, "I have all I need here among my own people." She left and Elisha asked Gehazi, "What can I do for her then?"

Gehazi replied, "She has no son and her husband is an old man."

Elisha called for her once again and she came up to his room and stood in the doorway as he said, "By this time next year you will be holding a son in your arms."

"Oh!" she exclaimed. "Please, sir, don't lie to me. You are a man of God." But she soon found out that he was not lying. She became pregnant and the next year she gave birth to a beautiful son as Elisha had said. The boy grew and one day, around harvest time the boy went out to the field to join his father and the other workers, when suddenly he cried, "My head hurts! My head hurts!"

The father told a servant to carry the boy to his mother immediately. The wife held him in her lap until noon at which time he died. She carried him up to Elisha's room, placed him on the bed and closed the door behind her. She did not breathe a word of her son's death to her husband or any of the servants but called her husband and asked for a donkey so that she may go see Elisha the prophet. "Why today?" he asked. "It's not a special occasion." "That's all right," she said. So she saddled the donkey and left not stopping to talk to anyone along on the way.

Elisha saw her coming from a distance and sent Gehazi to meet her and ask what was wrong, but the Shunammite replied that everything was all right. When she reached Elisha she bowed before him. Gehazi was about to push her away when Elisha said, "Leave her alone! Something is troubling her and it has been hidden from me." She said to him, "Sir, did I ask you for a son? Didn't I tell you not to raise my hopes?"

Elisha immediately turned to Gehazi and said, "Hurry, take my staff and go. Don't stop to greet anyone you meet, and if anyone greets you, don't take the time to answer. Go straight to the house and hold my stick over the boy."

Shunammite refused to leave with Gehazi, so she and Elisha headed back together. Gehazi did exactly as Elisha had commanded, but the boy showed no sign of life. When Elisha arrived at the house he went into his room alone and started to pray to the Lord. Then he lay down on top the boy, placing his mouth, eyes, and hands over the boy's mouth, eyes, and hands. He felt the boy's body start to get warm. He got up and walked about the room and then went back and stretched himself over the boy once again. The boy sneezed seven times and then opened his eyes. Elisha called for Gehazi and told him to call the Shunammite. When she came in, Elisha told her to take her son. She fell at his feet with her face touching the ground then took her son and left.

"Now," My mom said after she had finished her story, "What do you get from that?" Autumn's hand shot up.

"Yes, Autumn," my mom said.

"Never lose faith in the Lord or doubt that the Lord always has a plan for your life," Autumn said.

"Exactly. We must always trust in God and have faith because he knows what he is doing."

"She had faith like a mustard seed like Jesus said in Matthew," Autumn said. "Wait…let me find the verse," She opened her bible and began to search through the pages. "Here it is, 'Because you have so little faith. Truly I tell you, if you have faith as small as a mustard seed, you can say to this mountain, 'Move from here to there,' and it will move. Nothing will be impossible for you,' Matthew 17:20. She had faith strong enough to move a mountain… or in her case, bring her son back to life. I want to have that kind of faith, mommy," Autumn said.

"Ask and you shall receive Autumn."

• • •

"Actually now that I think about it, I do remember you saying that you wanted to pray for faith like the Shunammite woman," I said to Autumn as I went to the cabinet and took out two cups for tea.

"Yes, and over the years he has blessed me with exactly that, faith. I am more and more thankful for it every day."

"Is that how you know that Claire will turn out okay?" I poured hot water into the cups.

"Yes, plus I saw what happened to her mom, she'll be fine. Give her some time to figure out what she wants to be and what she wants to do. You can't force her to God just as we couldn't force you. It has to be a decision that she makes on her own. Let

God draw her to him."

"I suppose…what kind of tea do you want?"

"Berry tea is fine if you have any."

I reached up into my white painted cabinets and pulled out a red box of flavored tea packages and searched until I found the one that my sister preferred the most. I placed lemon and sugar on the server then brought it over, placing it on the table and sat back down beside Autumn. "This is the last time I'll bring it up, but I'm so worried about her, she's only fourteen and she's already starting to skip school and hang out with people that she shouldn't."

My sister looked at me long and hard as she stirred the tea packet into her cup of hot water, "If I remember correctly you started being rebellious when you were two."

"What can I say? I'm the strong–willed child."

"Let me think," my sister said as she took a short sip from her hot tea, "what's the first memory I can remember about you being rebellious…ah yes. The car ride to the grocery store."

"Not that story again."

"Would you like to tell it or should I?"

I was considered to be the strong-willed child in my family, unlike my sister who was the compliant child. My dad always thought it was because I'm older than my sister, if by only two years…nevertheless; I envied her, but only a little. She was loved by our mother and father. She never got into any real trouble, except for getting fussed at from time to time, but nothing more. She was what I like to call, the favorite.

I can recall the first time my mother became angry with me for my disobedience. I was around the age of seven and my mother decided to go to the store one night to get the ingredients to make a pizza. My sister and I were in the backseat of my mom's silver four-door car. When we had reached the store, my mother told us to stay in the car while she went inside to grab a few things. She had parked beside the curb, which let us know that she wouldn't be in the store for very long."

"What are you doing? We're not supposed to be doing that," Autumn said next to me.

"Leave me alone. I'm having fun. You can draw with me if you want," I said. Ignoring her I used my finger to create drawings on the frost covered back window.

"I don't want to get into trouble," she said refusing to look at me any longer.

"You won't. Look," I said continuing to draw a star and a heart on the window, "it's a lot of fun."

"No, thank you."

"Fine, suit yourself."

Eight minutes or so later our mom returned. Getting in the car she looked in her rearview mirror and saw my, at least what I thought were, amazing drawings.

"Who drew on the window?" my mom said trying to take control of her temper.

My sister and I both bowed our heads in silence, refusing to make eye contact with her.

"Autumn," my mom asked, "who drew on the back window?" She, of course, asked Autumn instead of me. My sister feared my mother and punishment; Autumn was always the go to child. But she never said it was me, at least not with her mouth. She looked over at me, before looking back down at her lap again.

"Cecilia! What did I tell you about drawing on my windows! You know better, how many times do we have to go over this?"

"I'm sorry, Mommy."

"Sorry? Cecilia 'sorry' is not a word that you can continue to throw out so that you can avoid a punishment. And you will be punished."

"How?" I mumbled, "Another spanking?"

"Get out! Get out of my car right now!" My mom yelled back.

"You want me to get out?" I asked taken aback.

"I don't need someone that can't respect my rules inside my car. So get out!"

I didn't budge. I wasn't sure if she was serious or if it was a test. I mean, no mother would throw their own daughter out on the street, right, even if we were still in front of a grocery store? But the next thing I knew Mom opened her door, then came to the back of the vehicle to open mine, dragged me out, closed the door behind me, and left me there by the curb. She hopped back into that little silver car with my sister and drove off without me.

I sat there on the curb for what seemed like years, but in all reality, it was only about three minutes. My sister said she had been the one to convince my mother to turn back around for me, although I found out later that Mom never planned to leave me, she was trying to get me to be obedient. Those were the scariest three minutes of my life. I didn't envy my sister so much at the end of that day and I had never been more thankful to have her in my life.

"Good times, huh?" my sister said with a smirk on her face.

"Okay, okay, that's one time. And I learned from my mistakes."

"Did you now?" my sister asked with laughter in her eyes, "Bombing our junior high school is learning a lesson?"

"I forgot about that one."

When I got into my ninth grade year of junior high school, my family began to wonder what possessed me to do the things I did. One year while in junior high I did a very stupid thing. I wrote, *"An explosive bomb will blow up the school in three weeks on March 16, there is no way to stop it"* on a stall of the girls' school bathroom. I really wasn't going to bomb my school, but the teachers, principals, and janitors didn't know that. I told one of my best friends, thinking that she would find it funny, but she betrayed me and soon the entire school knew what I'd done.

"Cecilia, do you know anything about the bomb threat that was found on the stall of the girls' restroom last week?" The principal had asked after calling me into his office one morning.

"There was a bomb threat?" I asked innocently. "No, sir, I had no idea."

"And you have no idea why your name was heard around the school as the guilty party?"

"No, sir. I would never do such a thing."

Word continued to spread after that and soon reached the ears of my sister. I still recall very clearly how she said she defended me with every fiber of her being.

"Hey, Autumn, I heard your sister is the one who's going to

bomb the school," an ex-friend of hers said one day during lunch.

"What are you talking about? My sister didn't write that," she said defensively.

"Well, that's what I heard," the ex-friend mocked.

"Listen. I don't care what you heard. My sister would never do such a stupid thing. And anyone who thinks otherwise does not know her. Cecilia would never threaten to blow up our school!"

"Okay, sorry I brought it up," the girl said walking off.

Needless to say, she was the most betrayed out of everyone when she found out the truth of my actions. Her bitterness towards me overpowered that of my parents, teachers, principals, and classmates.

I had been bullied by some of the popular kids in my school. They called me names, told me I wasn't smart…things like that. I hid this fact from my parents and my anger only built up towards them. I wanted them to suffer as I did. I wanted to scare them. So one day I asked to be excused from class for a bathroom break, my teacher agreed, I left and in my anger made a stupid decision.

"Don't start with me Autumn, I know, I know…I went to a juvenile detention center afterward as my punishment."

"Don't forget that you went for six weeks."

"I know."

"Then there was the time you had your pregnancy scare."

"What is this, a walk down memory lane?"

"I want to remind you of the stuff that you did. Put yourself in mom's and dad's shoes…now you know how they felt when you were out gallivanting around town and they had no idea where you were."

"I know…I know."

"Maybe you do, but we're not done yet. Now where were we? Ah yes, the pregnancy scare."

My first year in college I lost my virginity to the first boy who would have me and then to a few others after that. I didn't believe that my mom would ever find out that I was sleeping around, but somehow she knew. Even if she didn't know already she soon found out. By the time I had slept with the third guy, I took a test to find out I was pregnant. Well,…it's easy to say that 'scared' didn't even begin to express how I felt. I knew who the father was, but after our one night stand together I never saw him again. Eventually, I approached one of my friends about the matter and it scared her enough to call on my church pastor…who hours later called on my parents. No one seemed to be surprised by my actions at this time in my life. I guess they all expected it at this point. My mom said the Holy Spirit had revealed to her my doings. My dad shook his head in response, and my sister offered to throw me a baby shower. Autumn's words were, "Just because you're suffering doesn't mean your baby needs to do the same." Thankfully, however, my mom took me to Wal-Mart after this and bought a few more pregnancy tests as a precaution and I failed them all. It was a false positive. I thanked God that day for allowing me to not to be pregnant.

"Well for a short time, I seemed to turn my life around."

"God knew your heart, he knew that you were putting on false pretenses for family and friends, we all did. Except those who lived outside our family, they actually believed that you were turning over a new leaf.

"That's because at that point in my life all mom and dad had to punish me were threats to throw me out. I had friends who cared about me and if I needed to I could live with them."

"And we all saw how well that worked out, didn't we?"

"Yeah, they ditched me six months later after I got caught stealing over five hundred dollars from my job. Then I spent next three months in the Texas county jail."

"Your friends deserted you and the only ones you could depend on were your family, well for the most part. I think by that time everyone had lost faith in you."

"But you never did, why?" I asked as I took a sip from my now warm peach tea.

"Because I knew that one day you would find your way back to the Lord and be forgiven of the sins you had committed, and you soon did. Now you're married, following, Jesus and you were blessed with an amazing child."

"Thanks to you."

"Excuse me?"

"Autumn if it wasn't for the book that you wrote I'm not sure if I ever would have allowed Jesus to find me. When I started to read your book God began to speak to me through those pages immediately. Suddenly everything began to click. Everything I had always known, learned and had stored up in the back of my brain began to flow to the front and I instantly remembered everything I had tried so hard to forget. It still amazes me that my eyes were opened through the one person who never truly lost faith in me."

"You finally found the point in this memory lane process."

"What's that?"

"Never lose faith, even in your daughter. She's going to need someone in her life as well, to pick up the pieces and help her through the obstacles that she will face. She can't do that alone… neither could you."

"That's why you're my very own Shunammite woman and I am blessed to have you in my life," I reached over and gave Autumn a hug.

"Glad to be of service."

"So what do I pray so that God will help me with Claire?"

"Pray for patience, strength, wisdom and to have faith like a mustard seed," my sister said as she took one last sip from her berry tea.

I Always See Red

I always see red.
When I see red I roll my eyes and groan.
When I see red I can never seem to leave my bed.
When I see red my clothes no longer seem to be my own.

Once, I didn't see red.
"So full of life, so full of energy" my mother said.
"Come run with me," my brother said.
I didn't hesitate, and ran until the sun disappeared.

One time I didn't see red. It seems like such a distant dream.
It always comes unexpectedly and takes me by surprise.
Those days are not my own. But I'm free to do whatever I choose,
at least for today. God only knows what tomorrow holds.

I could see red.
I always see red.

Dear Mr. Chasey,

I am always reminded of you, on rare occasions that go unspoken.
I remember the first time I was sent to the hospital for surgery,
I woke up from my anesthetic slumber to the sound of the nurse
saying your name.

"Mr. Chasey," she said, "It's time for you to wake up. Please wake up."
She threatened to take you off your oxygen, but you didn't care.
You didn't take her threats seriously. Maybe you knew she was lying.

She threatened to leave your side, but again you didn't mind.
What were you dreaming about?
Were you dreaming about being at home, instead of the hospital?
Maybe you were somewhere near a quiet lake?

The nurse continued, unaware that I had woken from my anesthetic
slumber. Silently I prayed for you to wake up.
"Please Mr. Chasey, please wake up. I want to go back to sleep."
My prayers were soon answered.

You reached out for your nurse as your eyes remained closed
and asked for a cup of orange juice.
She laughed and took you off of your oxygen.

The nurse beside me realized I was awake and took me from the room.
That's the last I ever heard of you.
Mr. Chasey, why didn't you wake up sooner?
I might have been able to go back to sleep.

Handcuffed (A Life Sentence)

I looked at the man sitting behind the large desk. Glancing nervously at the floor, I listened as he talked. I should never have come. This was a big mistake. I have always obeyed the law and tried to do what was right. I was the one who people looked up to, wanted to be like. Yet here I am. How did this happen? I hung my head in shame. Everyone told me I was living the perfect life. I suppose it was…for a while. Then things started to change. I… started to change. He…started to change. No one ever expects things like this to happen, not to two people who love each other. Marriage is supposed to be lovely and easy…with a few struggles here and there. But after the honeymoon phase had ended, things start to get heated. He never abused me in any form and I never believed he was cheating on me…not once. It was all the yelling every night when he got home from work. His constant insults that there were women out there who would be glad to have it as good as I had it. It was the lack of intimacy every night that started to bother me, and the selfishness of not wanting to start a family until he was ready. What happened to the man I married? I thought I knew him. I thought I knew me, but after three years, I couldn't take it anymore. So I did the only rational thing I could possibly think of…and that's why I'm in the place I am now. After talking to me for a short time, the man behind the large mahogany desk seemed to have come to his conclusion. Getting out of his black swivel computer chair he came over to me and asked me to stand up. This man could pass for a TV detective, you know the kind, the ones that wear a black coat, white starched dress shirt, black tie, and faded black slacks. He looked at me sternly as he started to clasp a heavy silver bracelet onto my left wrist.

The day that we were married our pastor stated that we were entering into bondage…a covenant that was permanent. Pastor David talked about marriage and commitment, but all too soon he was finished. The best man handed him the ring and my husband nervously struggled to place the wedding ring on my outstretched finger. My mother removed the blue flowered tissue enclosed inside our wedding programs to wipe the tears that were flowing down her neatly made-up face. My father fixed his gaze on me as if to remind himself that he was losing his baby girl. My sister bent down to adjust my long flowing veil from where it had blown in the wind. The pastor said, "I now pronounce you husband and wife," and a bluebird or two crossed over our heads as we leaned into to share our first kiss as a married couple. Our wedding day was amazing. There was dancing, laughter, delicious food, family, friends, and lots of love. But my wedding day went as quickly as it had arrived. All the decorations were soon taken down and placed neatly away, never to be seen again. We'd spent so much time planning and preparing for our wedding day, that we never took the time to think about how important it was to prepare for our marriage. We had been counseled for six months, but so much of that information didn't seem to apply to us. We thought our life to be like our wedding day, a constant celebration. We had forgotten that though our wedding would end in a flash, our marriage would last a lifetime.

Two days ago I approached the pastor of my church to get advice on how to fix my marriage. Michael was working as usual, so I went to confront my pastor to see if I could obtain enough information to fix my marriage.

"Tara how are you doing today?" my pastor asked when he opened up the door to his private office.

"I am well Pastor David, how are you?" I said sitting in one of the high-backed chairs.

"Where is Michael today?"

"He's at work, as usual."

"I see. Well, what can I help you with today?"

"My marriage."

"Your marriage? Are you and Michael having problems?"

"In a word, yes."

"Shouldn't he be here trying to save your marriage as well?"

"I'm not even sure he realizes our marriage is on the brinks."

"Why do you think that?"

"About a year after we were married, he started to spend more time at work. He said that bills had to be paid and that he had a chance for a promotion."

"You didn't believe him?"

"I did, but then the hours he spent away from home became longer and when he returned late at night from work he would complain about the long hours and how he felt wore out. I asked why he was spending so much time at work if he didn't like it, but he said that it was his duty to provide for his family. After that, anytime I mentioned how he could change the way he did *anything* we would argue and he would say I shouldn't question his authority as a husband."

"After about a year, most marriages usually experience a shift as couples become more at ease with each other. The honeymoon period ends and the challenges of everyday life begin. Some couples want the "happily ever after", but there is no happily ever after. Marriage is not a fairytale. It is real life walked out on a day to day basis. What day do you think would work best for you and Michael to come see me together?"

"He's off some Saturdays and usually every Sunday."

"Here's what I would like you to do. I want both of you to attend church this Sunday as usual and pay close attention to the message. Then I want you and Michael to come to my office next Saturday morning at eight and I will give both of you instructions on how to work on fixing your marriage."

"Thank you, Pastor David," I said rising from my chair. "We will be here."

I stayed up waiting for him to get home. He was late as usual. He barely noticed me lying on the couch with the TV on when he entered the living room from the garage.

"How was work?" I asked not moving from my spot on the couch.

"Wha—? Oh hey. What are you still doing up?"

"I was waiting on you. I need to talk to you about something?"

"Can it wait? I'm tired…exhausted…and not in the mood tonight. Alright?" He began to walk past me as he headed towards the bedroom.

"I talked to Pastor David today," I yelled behind him. I shifted into a seated position on the couch.

"Did you now? Why did you do that?" he stopped in his tracks.

"I figured that he might be able to help us with the problems we're having in our marriage."

"What problems?"

"What problems? Michael, we never see each other anymore. You're always working, we never go out on dates or spend any alone time together. And I don't think that you've even realized that I'm thinking about going to work again because I'm so bored here at the house during the day."

"First of all, I told you that I'm up for a promotion. That comes first. Secondly, I can't help it if you want to have a date night every weekend, we can talk about that in the months to come. And thirdly, if you get so bored during the day I don't know why you don't join a wives club or a book club of some sort. But hey if it suits your fancy, go get a job…I don't care."

"You don't care. That's good to know…no really…thanks for that."

"What do you want me to say, Tara? I'm not apologizing for the decisions I make for my household."

I got up from the couch, allowing my nightgown to fall to the floor, and walked past him. "Pastor David told us to pay close attention to the sermon on Sunday and then we have an appointment with him next Saturday," I said ending our conversation.

"Next Saturday? Tara, you know that I don't control my schedule. I might have to work that day."

"That's not my problem…I'm sure you'll figure something out."

Sunday morning we did as Pastor David suggested and attended the first service at our church. He began to talk about marriage and the problems they face today.

"Recent surveys say that sixty percent of marriages for couples between the ages of twenty and twenty-five end in divorce," Pastor David began.

Looking at the statistics flash on the screen captured my attention. I was 23 and Michael was on the verge of turning 26. Would my marriage to Michael become another statistic? Before our wedding we vowed that divorce would never be in our vocabulary, but what about now? Have our thoughts changed towards the subject?

During the sermon, I noticed that Michael received several emails, text messages, and muted phone calls. Although he tried to pay attention to the pastors' sermon, the interruptions distracted us both from listening to the sermon. I faintly heard the pastor say, "The second the husband and wife say I do, is the second they become handcuffed to their marriage partner."

Saturday morning Michael and I showed up at the church for our eight o'clock counseling session. We entered into the pastor's office and after greeting us and offering coffee, Pastor David began to speak.

"Michael, you and Tara are here today to fix your marriage, correct?" we nodded in unison as he continued, "Marriage is a journey and you can make it easy or hard. If you two don't learn how to walk together, you make it hard and it will hurt. Not only will you hurt your marriage, but yourselves and the way you look at one another. If you learn to walk together your journey will become a lot less painful. You see marriage is like a symphony, the two of you must learn to work together in unison to bring forth a perfect harmony."

"So what is it you suggest we do pastor?" I asked looking over at Michael who was checking his cell phone every few seconds.

"I suggest that for the next twelve hours you both learn how to work together," he said as he began to open up his office desk drawer and pull out something silver. "I suggest that we put my sermon from Sunday into effect."

Getting out of his black swivel computer chair he came over to Michael and me and asked us to stand. He looked at me sternly as he started to clasp a heavy silver bracelet onto my left wrist and then the other half onto Michaels' right wrist.

"This may seem a little odd, but I believe you both need a lesson in communication and compromise. So," he said clapping his hands together loudly, "for the next twelve hours you will literally become 'one'. You will learn how to walk, move, and flow together as a married couple. Yes, you will have your problems, but I trust that you can figure them out together. I will keep the key here with me and at eight o'clock tonight the both of you will return and we will see how well everything worked out."

"What if we come back tonight and we haven't worked out our issues," I asked.

"Until the two of you have worked out your problems you will remain handcuffed. We'll just pray that it won't take you that long, because if you don't work out your problems you will be the ones suffering, not me."

"Are you sure this will work?"

"The only way to learn to walk together is by actually working together. I have faith that the two of you will sort out your issues. So I'll send you on your way and I will see both of you tonight at eight," Pastor David said as he walked us over to the door, "Remember to show love, patience, and kindness towards one another," he said closing the door behind us.

With our handcuffs on we walked out to Michaels' Silver Ford F-150. He opened the driver's side door and looked down at our wrists that were linked together.

"Well, this is an utter waste of time. I could be at work right now, but instead, I'm —"

I rolled my eyes as he complained and began to crawl from the driver's side seat to the passenger seat pulling Michael behind me, landing my thigh hard on the armrest in between the two seats in the process.

"Would you stop pulling my wrist? We're supposed to be working together remember. This was, after all, your idea."

"Yes, it was my idea. But if we were working as a team from the beginning we wouldn't be in this situation," I said pointing to the handcuffs as they gleamed from the reflection from the sun as if mocking us.

Driving was the first part of our test as a recently handcuffed married couple. Michael couldn't very well drive with his left hand. He's right handed so it was really difficult for him to drive when his right hand was attached to my left. He tried driving with his left hand, but his turns almost put us into a ditch. We settled for driving with both of his hands on the steering wheel and my left hand loosely holding onto his right.

"I can't wait to get home," he stated.

"Why are you thinking about leaving me? I'm not sure how well that will work out," I said shaking the silver bracelet in the air. "We're attached at the wrist remember."

"Shut up! And move your hand." He removed his hand from mine and forced my hand into my lap causing the truck to swerve from the left lane to the right in a matter of seconds."

"What the heck are you doing? Are you crazy! We could've been killed."

"Stop over exaggerating."

"I don't know how he expects me to deal with *this* for twelve hours." I lightly returned my hand to his as we drove the rest of the way home in silence.

We pulled into our driveway, and all I wanted to do was flee to my art studio in our basement to have some alone time. Michael opened up the driver side door and pulled on my arm as he tried to exit. I was immediately brought back to reality and remembered that for the next twelve hours I would not get a single second of privacy.

"Are you trying to yank my arm off?" I asked rubbing the slowly reddening skin around my wrist.

"Sorry."

"Apology not accepted," I joked as I climbed over the armrest into the drivers' seat and out of the truck.

"Tara…"

"Listen…Pastor David said that the only way this would work is if we compromise and work together. So I think for the next eleven hours or so, we should put our differences behind us," I said closing the truck door behind me.

"I suppose."

"The least you can do is try."

"I'll try. But the next time that we need marital advice, I suggest that we do it my way," Michael said with a sly smile.

"And what way is that?"

"I'm not quite sure at the moment. But I can assure you that it's better and smarter than this."

I didn't want our marriage to become a statistic and have our relationship end in divorce, but this is not what I expected. I trust Pastor David and believe that he wants all marriages to survive, but was this going a little too far? He has helped to save many marriages in the past, so I believe that he is doing what he believes is best. I sighed with resignation and told myself to trust that this would work.

We walked into the house closing our garage door behind us, soon making our way to the bedroom and over towards our four-poster bed. The coolness of the satin sheets felt inviting, as I ran my hands over the sheets. Tears stung my eyes as disappointment flowed over me.

We sat in silence for a while before Michael looked over at the clock that hung above our bedpost. In the middle of the clock was a quote that read, "Love conquers all" a gift from my dad at our wedding shower. I wonder if my dad knew that we would be going through the bondage that came with marriage sooner than we thought.

"Listen, I know this is probably not the way you thought this would turn out," Michael said quietly.

I nodded in agreement.

"But if I have to be handcuffed to anyone, I'm glad it's you."

"Cliché much?" I asked laughing.

"Why don't we cook some breakfast?" Michael suggested.

We got up together and walked into the kitchen. I've always liked my kitchen. The layout of the kitchen is what convinced me to choose this house. It was an open design with dark green marble countertops, and solid black cabinets. The island included a small sink and overhead storage for pots and pans.

We walked over to the sink and tried to wash our hands. Washing and drying our hands while handcuffed wasn't the easiest task. and we both ended up with our hands still a little damp.

"So what are you in the mood for?" I asked.

"Pancakes?"

"Okay, you get the batter and I'll get the eggs," I started to walk over to the refrigerator as Michael walked over to the dry goods cabinet.

"Ow!" we yelled at the same time.

"Okay, let's try this again," Michael said rubbing his wrist, "We can get the pancake mix first then we can get all of the refrigerated items next."

After gathering all the items we worked as a team getting our pancakes, eggs, and sausage fixed.

As Michael began to stir the pancake mix, I tried my best to crack open the eggs with one hand. Everything was going smoothly until he reached over the sink to put some more water in a cup. My hand went with his, while the egg I was holding flew out of my left hand and fell onto the floor. I stepped into the cracked egg yolk and fell to the floor. Michael came with me, but only after bracing himself as much as he could by grabbing the bowl of pancake mix. The bowl went up into the air and found a nice spot on the top of his face.

"Real smooth Tara," Michael laughed as the pancake batter began to fall into his mouth.

I couldn't help but to laugh, "How does it taste?"

"Why don't you try some?" he asked as he threw a large glob at my face.

"Real mature," I said back to him as I picked up some of the cracked egg yolks and threw it at his face.

"Talk about mature. Come on…let's clean this up," he laughed as he grabbed my hand to help me up. Neither of us noticed that my foot was still in a large portion of the spilled yolk and I immediately fell back to the ground causing him to fall forward right on top of me. "Are you okay?" he asked as batter dripped off his face and onto mine.

"We have got to stop meeting like this. What would my mom think?" I said with a laugh.

"Who cares? She really never liked me much anyway," he joked.

"You know as well as I do, that that's not true."

I watched as his eyes roamed from my eyes to my lips, "She especially never liked it when I kissed you in front of her."

"Well then, it's a good thing she's not here at the moment."

"Yes, it is," he said as he mouth quickly fell onto mine. His kiss was so tender and passionate that it took me by surprise. I felt his kiss, his touch all throughout my body. It was as if I was being kissed by him for the first time all over again. "Come on," he said withdrawing his lips from mine, "let's get this kitchen cleaned up."

We cleaned slowly as we joked, laughed, and threw excess food at one another. After a long while had passed we eventually had the kitchen cleaned and two plates steaming with food.

We sat down together at the table, Michael sitting at the head of the table and me sitting to his right. We ate our pancakes, sausage, and eggs in silence until Michael spoke.

"We haven't spent this much time together in some time."

"I know," I said softly as I continued to eat.

"I saw a show once about Siamese twins. They were joined on the side and had to do everything together, but they were very different. One colored her hair red and the other one was blonde."

I eyed him for a moment, "That has always been one of the things I always loved most about you. Your interest and knowledge of the most unusual facts," I said trying to hide a smile.

Michaels' cell phone rang and he reached to answer it, this time remembering that he should use his left hand.

"Yeah...okay. Thanks for the reminder," he said as he ended the call.

"What was that about?" I asked curiously.

"I forgot that the Awards dinner is tonight."

"That's tonight? I thought it was next weekend."

"Nope, it's tonight. I know you said that you didn't want to go, but since we're handcuffed..." his words trailed off.

"What time does it start? Five o'clock right? Well, we better get ready soon," I said looking at my watch that read 12:05.

"Why do we need to get ready so soon?"

"We're handcuffed, Michael. Do you have any idea how hard it will be to get dressed?"

"Tara I didn't mention it to you, but I'm almost positive they will ask me to take the job as director of my department."

"Director? But that will mean you will be here even less than you are now."

"I know."

"Are you going to take it?"

"Only if you agree. I can't do it without you and your support."

"No, Michael. You cannot put me on the spot like this. You have to decide."

"Well then...that's why I told them no."

At four thirty we began to head out to Michaels' dinner. It took us three hours to dress. We both had to shower to get the egg yolk and pancake batter off of us. Then we had to dress...putting on pants, shoes, and make-up was not at all complicated. Because I needed something simple yet elegant to wear, Michael suggested I wear the black strapless dress he had given me for our anniversary last year. We pinned one of my elegant shawls around my shoulders and the ensemble was complete. It was a bit more complicated for Michael to find a shirt that he could fit in due to the cuffs. As a last resort, we decided to cut off his right sleeve and sew it back up once it was on his arm, which sounds a lot easier than it actually was. But thankfully we were able to get in contact with my mom and due to her amazing sewing skills; we eventually got the job done. All she could do was laugh at the two of us as we walked and worked together as one, saying it was the funniest thing she had ever seen. As we drove to the party my left hand was once again on top of his right and the handcuffs dug into my skin as my body leaned with the car whenever Michael made a left turn. By the time we arrived my left arm was aching with pain.

Many of Michael's coworkers and friends greeted us as we entered and commented about the handcuffs. Several men teased him about being brave enough to actually allow the experiment. Some of the women thought it was a great idea, but said their husbands would never go through with it. After finding our table, we went over to the buffet and fixed ourselves a plate. After our breakfast trial run, we really began to move as one. We returned to our seats and began to eat, as Michael introduced me to several more members of his team. Everyone spoke highly of my husband and his employees told me story after story of his hardworking dedication and how he never let a second go by without bringing up his lovely wife.

Finally, the CEO of the hospital, Gene Rivers, stood up to speak. He spoke about how he appreciated each person's hard work, commitment, and dedication. He said that one of the promotions they were announcing for the night, included a hard working dedicated person who had been chosen to be the director of IT department. "Michael Oliver. We just want to say Congratulations! Come. Come." Everyone hollered, "Speech! Speech!"

Michael arose and walked onto the stage with me behind him. Gene handed Michael the microphone and stepped back.

"Thank you Gene, and thank you, everyone, who made this day possible. It is an honor to receive this promotion," Michael said as he moved over to the podium, pulling me behind him. My wrist hurt so I adjusted the cuff on my wrist and stood beside him as he continued to talk, "I started at this company three years ago. I have come a long way, and it has been a hard journey. Several times I wanted to call it quits, but I made a commitment to stay regardless of the difficulties. I could not have done it without my wife. She has had to put up with my long hours at work, being home alone and a waking up and going to bed with a grumpy husband. She has been there for me and always encourages me no matter what. Without her, I would not be here. Work is important, but we must never forget those who are at home waiting for us. So as much as I would like to take this new position, I..."

It was in that split second while he was addressing co-workers and supervisors that the realization hit me. This was his life, our life. As a wife, I needed to be there to support my husband by lifting him up and not putting him down. I should be his cheerleader and encourage him when he comes home from a long day at work. He doesn't want to hear more griping and complaining from me when he enters into his house. As a wife, it was my job to submit to my husband, be there for him, and to love him. And I did love him, so why did I want to take something away from him that he loved so much. If by him taking this promotion meant making him dinner at two in the morning, I would do it gladly. Our home should be his place of refuge away from the turmoil of his work. He was doing his job as a husband; it was time for me to do my job as a wife.

I looked over at him, smiled and nodded my head as I mouthed, "Accept it." He paused and frowned at me as I said, "I want you to do this for you...for us." As I looked at him, his eyes began to sparkle. I saw the same love and tenderness in his eyes I had seen on our wedding day, but somehow this time, it was different.

"Thank you," he said as he took my hand and held it gently. "I appreciate the confidence you have in me. I will not let you down." Although he was addressing the audience, I knew he was talking to me. We walked down the stairs and off stage as I realized the look Michael gave me was not the look of a newly married man, but of a man who knew all his wife's faults, and loved her anyway. His look towards me said, *I'm here for you, you're safe with me, and I'm never letting you go.*

Several people came over to greet us, congratulate Michael on his promotion, and compliment his speech. He never let go of my hand. People came up to him but he thanked and greeted each one with his left hand. As everyone began to leave, I turned to face him.

"Michael, I want to apologize. I never realized everything you had done for me. I didn't understand why you worked all day and seldom took the time to spend with me. I was stubborn and selfish. I wanted you all to myself, but tonight I realized that I can't always have that. Your work is important and I have to grow accustomed to the fact that I must share you with others."

"I'm sorry too Tara. I do spend too much time at work, and with my new promotion, I'm going to use the hours that they don't need me to be at home with you. You are my wife and you should come before my job. Somehow I've forgotten that along the way. Forgive me?"

"Only if you forgive me."

"Let's go home," Michael said as he pulled me close to kiss me lightly on the cheek.

"I'll go wherever you go."

Tell Me

Tell me again the story of the girl who found love.
How long did she wait?
Did she ever doubt that her prince would come?

Tell me again about how they first met.
Was it love at first sight?
Or were they friends long before?

Tell me again how she looked on her wedding day.
Did he cry as she walked to him?
Did she fear for the night that would follow?

Tell me again how she felt holding her newborn baby.
Did she cry as she held him?
Did she name him after his father?

Tell me again how she died at his side.
Did he kiss her one last time?
Did he promise to love her always?

Tell me again the story of a never ending love.

And More

The interlocking of fingers that a man and a woman in love share.
Perfect.

The way an old man still looks longingly at his wife.
Through all her wrinkles, baggage, age, and past life.
Love.

The way a newly married man gently carries his bride
over the threshold into her new life.
Breathless.

The way any man gently caresses her face slowly, carefully,
lovingly, and gently places a lingering kiss on the top of her forehead.
Beautiful.

I want that. *All* of that. And more.

The late night phone calls when she cannot sleep.
He is yawning and beyond exhausted, but still willing to listen.
Communication.

The first fight that is only the start of all fights.
But somehow, someway they work through them.
Life.

The cry of the first baby that appears out of her womb.
The love that develops in both of their eyes.
Patience.

The time when you know, that you know, and they know.
That this is the person they are going to spend the rest of their life with.
They have found their, *The One.*
Timing.

I want that. *All* of that. And more.

LOUD DREAMS, SILENT LIFE

I jumped into my bed and turned on the TV to catch the last showing of "Gilligan's Island" for the night.

"Grace, did you forget something?" my mom signed as she entered my bedroom.

"I don't think so," I signed back.

"The pills that Dr. Torres prescribed for you?"

I let out a long breath. "Do I have to? I had two yesterday."

She touched my head as if checking to see if I had a fever, then signed, "Are you still having the headaches?"

"Maybe."

She cocked her head to one side and looked at me closely, "Grace..."

"...I am."

"Then yes you have to. Doctors' orders, two a day until the headaches go away," she chuckled at her rhyme. She handed me two of the pills and a cup of water and watched as I popped the pills into my mouth and swallowed. "Gilligan again? Really, Grace. This must be the first season since it's in black & white."

"It's the one when Gilligan finds a stone and makes three wishes on it."

"Is that so?" Mom signed, "And what does he wish for, to get off the island?"

"Not exactly."

"Never mind," she laughed. "It's time for bed, so one episode, and then lights out."

"Yes, ma'am," I signed. I embraced her, feeling the touch of her lips as they brushed against my cheek. "Goodnight."

"And you'd have your choice of leading ladies to pick from." The captions read as Ginger spoke.

"Oh yeah I would," Gilligan replied.

"And who would you pick?"

"You know who."

"I know, but tell me anyway," she said smiling.

"Lassie."

"Oh Gilligan, you're terrible!"

"Oh Gilligan," I said smiling to myself as I closed my eyes and fell asleep.

I awoke on a bench and began to look around as I sat up. Where was I? Nothing here looked familiar. Everything was in black and white. I felt as if I had shifted back into an old movie from the1960's.

"I must be in an episode of Gilligan's Island," I thought to myself.

An empty sidewalk stretched out in front of the bench and I looked around and saw no one. On the other side of the street, several buildings were lined up in a neat row. Everything seemed unreal or maybe just make-believe, like a Barbie world of sorts. Was this real or was it a play world made out of cardboard held together by disappearing purple glue? There was a strange silence. I didn't feel the wind on my face or see the trees blowing in the breeze. It appeared to have light, although I saw no sun. There wasn't a human being, animal, or vehicle in sight. Turning around to look at the unmoving scenery behind me, I caught a glimpse of some words engraved into the center of the bench, Effugio De Vita.

"Now would be the perfect time for a computer," I said aloud. I began to think I was in a lifeless dream from which I would never be awakened when I saw a young man exit from one of the cardboard buildings resembling a restaurant. "If this world is a strange relation to Gilligan's Island, then that man must be Gilligan…or the professor."

"Gilligan, Gilligan, over here!" I screamed to the man exiting the building.

"Hey, hey, stop yelling, you're going to wake up the whole town," the stranger yelled at me as he crossed the gray street, "And who the heck is Gilligan?"

"What town? There's no one here," I whispered, "And you don't know who Gilligan is?"

"That's because they're all trying to sleep, no thanks to you. Who are you anyway? How did you get here?" he asked ignoring my question about Gilligan.

"Who am I? Who are you?"

The young man was tall. He had short brown hair, wore a black church vest with a white undershirt and a black tie, with black slacks and appeared to be about nineteen. Like everything else I had seen so far, he appeared in black and white.

"How did you get here? We never get visitors in this town," he demanded.

"Why is that? Is it because everything is made out of cardboard?" I motioned to the building behind him that he had come from.

"What are you talking about? Those buildings aren't made of cardboard," he said rolling his eyes.

"Right…"

"I'm going to ask you again…how did you get here?"

"I don't know, I just did. I woke up on the bench."

"That bench?" he asked pointing to the bench behind me.

"Yes, why?" I asked looking at him curiously.

"Well, that bench is for visitors that come in on the bus. But as far as I know, the bus hasn't run in over sixty years. Did you come in on the bus?"

"I don't remember."

"Yes, or no, it's a simple question!"

"I don't know! You don't have to yell, I can hear y...wait…I can hear you."

"Congratulations," he said sarcastically.

"No...I can hear your...voice." Talking with this complete stranger had come so naturally to me that I hadn't realized that I could hear in this world.

"Thank you for stating the obvious."

"No, no, it's...forget it. You wouldn't understand," I said as I walked over to take a seat on the bench, "What's with the bus anyway?"

"The bus only comes when people are in need of an escape. I apologize for yelling at you, you surprised me that's all. We don't get many visitors. What's your name?"

"Grace."

"Nice to meet you, Grace, I'm Daniel. What are you escaping from?"

"Life, I suppose."

"Well, then, I guess it's my job to help you."

"Your job?"

"That's how it works here. Whoever finds the person in need of help first must help them to relax and free their mind from whatever they are escaping from.

An escape. Why would I make up a world to escape from the real world?

"You said something earlier about being able to hear me. What did you mean by that?" he said after a moment of silence.

"Short version? I'm deaf. Long version? When I was five I begged and pleaded with my parents until they finally agreed to enroll me into a dance class. I promised to help at home and keep my grades up, and I've been dancing ever since. Being shy, I used dancing and music to express myself and sometimes as an escape from my daily life. I love dancing. It was not only my passion but my life. I felt like I could do anything when I was on the dance floor."

"You said, 'was' not 'is'? Do you not dance anymore?"

"Not as much as I did. I lost my hearing three years ago. It's hard to dance when you can't hear the music. I tried for a time or two afterward, but it was never the same."

"What happened?"

"The doctors called it Sudden Deafness. They're not sure why, but I woke up one day and I couldn't hear anything. My mom took me to the doctor and he gave me a hearing test which I failed. The doctor said I had a loss of 40 decibels in three connected frequencies. He diagnosed it as SSHL or Sudden Hearing Loss. I was devastated. I didn't understand why it was happening to me. The doctor said more research has to be done on the issue. I had a slight return of my hearing before the end of the day, but it was gone again the next morning. I've been deaf ever since."

"How do you communicate with your family?"

"My mom took up Sign Language in high school. She received a master's degree in deaf education. My parents have been teaching my brother and me sign language since before we could talk. So it wasn't a hard transition in that area."

"Hmm…so how does a dancer stop dancing?"

"I didn't stop dancing altogether. I work in the dance class at my school as a teacher's aide and an alternate. I substitute whenever they need me, so I do dance, but not as passionately as before."

"Don't fear, Grace. Have faith and trust that God has a plan for your life. He wouldn't allow you to go deaf if he didn't think that you could handle it. You're stronger than you know," Daniel said.

"How do you know that?"

"Jeremiah 29:11 states, "For I know the plans I have for you," declares the LORD, "plans to prosper you and not to harm you, plans to give you hope and a future." God knows what he's doing. You only have to trust in him and he will see you through."

"Right…of course. I know that. Sometimes it's hard, though, trying to have faith when your whole world suddenly falls apart."

"Yes. But this is only God's way of testing you to see if you will fail or succeed. If you will have faith or deny him at the first chance you get. It's ultimately your ending decision."

I nodded, "Well I haven't denied him so far, and I don't plan on starting now."

"That's great!"

"Umm…has…has that rainbow always been there?" I asked pointing into the far distance.

He looked off to the right of the buildings and saw a rainbow that was breathtaking. "Yes, it has always been there."

"Are you sure?" I asked noticing that he was now in color as well. He had short brown hair and dark brown eyes that complimented his tan skin complexion well.

He looked at me and smiled. "You're only now seeing it because your hope has been restored. After you've been here for quite some time, you will realize that you won't need an escape anymore and your time here will be complete."

"When will that be?"

"When everything that you see around you is alive and in color."

Beep…Beep… Beep…Beep

I opened my eyes to see my mom. "It's time to get up Grace," she mouthed.

"Mom," I signed, "I had a weird dream."

I told my Mom about the dream then asked, "Mom, do you know what Effugio De Vita means?" I signed as I sat up in my bed.

"I don't, but I bet the internet does," she signed as she began to look it up on her iPhone, "It's Latin for Escape from Life."

Later that night I had another dream about Daniel.

"Hi! Good to see you again." Daniel said when I showed up beside him on the bench.

"Hi," I said looking around the black and white town curiously, "were you waiting for me?"

"Yes. I thought you might come back into town today. I haven't been waiting long, however, you were right. You definitely did not show up on the bus…which is odd."

"How so?"

"Everyone who comes here in need of an escape shows up on the bus. And when they are in no longer need of an escape they leave on the bus. You, just kind of pop-up out of nowhere. Which makes me a tad curious…"

"Curious about what?"

"It doesn't matter. So, how was your day today?"

"It was nice. Today was Sunday so my family and I went to church. Then my mom and I went shopping. Afterward, we came back to the house for family movie night. It was actually a very relaxing day."

"Are you pretty close with your family?"

"I am. I love them so much. I wouldn't have been able to get through my sudden deafness without them by my side. My mom comforted me, my dad made me laugh to get through the pain, and my brother…well he's still really young, but he does what he can," I smiled to myself.

"What about your friends?"

"I actually lost a couple of them after the incident. They weren't sure how to treat me afterward, that or they weren't sure how to communicate with me anymore. My mom eventually suggested that I change schools, which I was happy about. I like it there a lot, and it's nice being around people who are going through the same things as me. Although some of them were actually born deaf. I do, however, keep in contact with two of my friends from my old school. I guess that's one way to tell who your real friends are, huh? Just lose your hearing. Lose one identity and gain another."

"You didn't lose an identity. You only gained another one in return. Plus, when you lose one sense, your other senses are heightened," he said as I nodded in reply.

"What about you?"

"What about me?"

"What do you do here in this black and white/colorful world when you're not helping confused teenagers."

"To be honest, this is my first time. The way it works here is that everybody gets one person to help and after they have finished helping their person…they move on. There are many friends and family members that I had a while back, but whom I haven't seeen in years. Once you finish…you're gone."

"Wait…what? Who made that rule?"

He shrugged and looked sadly off into the distance.

"Where do they move on to?" I asked following his gaze.

"I wish I knew."

"Well, that's depressing. How did you get here in the first place?"

"I was born here," he turned to look at me and smiled, "Right over there beyond those buildings. Would you like to see?"

I nodded as I followed him from the bench, passed the black

and white buildings, and over to a small cottage that sat in the middle of a small circle of pine trees.

"This is it. It's not much, but it still holds a lot of great memories for me."

"It's been boarded up," I commented. It was a small light brown bricked home, with a chimney. It almost resembled that of a children's playhouse, because it was so quaint and cute. But the windows and doors had been boarded. That's when I noticed that the house and trees were in color.

"Yes, no one has lived here in years. My mom left when I was seven and my dad left a year later."

"Because they were helping the people that came in on the bus?"

He nodded. "I went to live with my aunt and uncle shortly after that. They never left. They didn't want to leave me while I was still in my teens. I was thankful for that. If they would have left I would have been an orphan by the age of ten, if not younger."

"Where are they now?"

"They're around."

"Thank you for showing me this. It helps to put things back in perspective for me."

"What sort of things?"

"The small things. Here I am crying and going crazy over the fact that I don't have my hearing anymore when you lost your parents at such a young age." Even though I hardly knew Daniel, his story broke my heart. I watched as my arms went around his body and brought him into a tight hug. Only a second had passed before he returned my hug. His hug was nice and warm. I felt safe, comforted, and peaceful. After a few minutes had passed I withdrew from him and apologized.

"There's no need for an apology. I needed a hug as much as you did. Thank you."

"I do what I can."

He laughed as he began to walk back towards the bench, "Yes I can see that."

"Will I see you again tomorrow?" I asked as we approached the bench.

"I believe so. Unless God has another plan in mind."

I heard a beep beginning to sound in my ears and I knew that it was my time to leave. "Until next time."

The next afternoon I was walking towards the kitchen and saw my Mom and Dad having an intense conversation. I would usually hide out in the hallway to eavesdrop in on their conversation, but since I couldn't hear them I grabbed the nearest pair of ears close to me.

"Benjamin, what are mom and dad talking about?" I asked my little brother.

"You know it's not polite to eavesdrop, Gracie," he said in his high pitched four-year-old voice.

"I know, but I can't hear them…so I'm curious."

"You keep saying that you can't hear. Don't you have ears?" Benjamin asked.

"Yes Ben, I have ears."

"Then open them and eavesdrop on your own," he said and started to walk away.

"Whoa, there little buddy," I said grabbing him by the arm. "I have ears Ben, but mine don't work as well as yours do."

"Why not?"

"Because God took away one of my five senses to enhance my others. Since my hearing is gone, my sight, smell, taste, and touch have become much better. Here you try, close your eyes and try to focus on what mom and dad are saying."

"Wait, you're trying to trick me, aren't you?"

"I was, but apparently it's not going to work."

"Are you sure you can't hear?"

"I'm positive, Ben. I can't hear a thing."

"What about now? Can you hear me now Gracie?" Ben started to yell. This was something that Ben had started to do ever since I lost my hearing. I believe that a part of him hoped that if he yelled enough in my ear, I would eventually get my hearing back. But so far, it wasn't working.

I couldn't hear his voice, but his facial expressions as he tried to put emphasis onto every word he screamed made me laugh.

He bucked his eyes wide as he looked towards the kitchen and stifled a giggle. "Mom just yelled at me for yelling in the hallway. Did you hear her? Did you hear me?" he mouthed.

He got yelled at for yelling…well, there is your irony, I laughed to myself. "No, I didn't, but I read your lips perfectly," I whispered.

"Oh. I'm sorry, but don't worry, Gracie, God will give your hearing back eventually. Maybe he'll take away your sense of taste to make it even," he said as he laughed and ran towards his room.

Shaking my head at my brother I turned my attention back to the conversation in the kitchen. I wasn't able to catch everything, but reading lips was something I was beginning to do well.

"Why would she need a psychiatrist?" my Dad was asking.

"Aren't you worried, John? You know that Grace's dreams have a tendency to come true," my Mom said.

"I know that, but a psychiatrist? What will that help?"

"What will it hurt? I'm scared for her John. She's been dreaming about this 1960's dream world and that boy for the past two days."

"It's a dream," Dad said, "So what?"

"Do I need to remind you of all the dreams she has had that have come true? It's as though she goes to sleep and when she wakes up the dreams come to life. Like the time she dreamed someone from your job stabbed you in the back and a week later you were fired while you were out on sick leave. Or when she dreamed she had a car, although she did not know we planned to surprise her with it the next day and when she dreamed Minnie was going to have a baby boy…a year before she even got pregnant."

"There's no need to get shaken up over something as small as this, Claire. We have to have faith that God knows what he's doing… he has a plan. He always does."

One Week and Twelve Pills Later

"Hey Grace, did you see Daniel again last night?" Carmen signed.

Carmen became my friend almost immediately when I transferred to Gallaudet University. She's a CODA (Child of a Deaf Adult) and one of the main students on campus who has helped me feel like I belonged, she's helped my recent transition to a deaf school to be a lot smoother than when I first transferred. She was the only one who seemed to be quite fascinated by my dreams.

"I wish I could meet him. I wish for only one day, you and I could switch dreams…that way I'd finally know what it feels like to hear for a night and have a Romeo and Juliet type of romance. I would never wake up!"

"Really Carmen? Daniel and I are nothing like them. Plus, we're just friends," I signed back.

"Right. Oh and his name…! Is he gorgeous? I bet he's gorgeous? Did you ever figure out how you got those dreams? Because I would give almost…"

Carmen was 5'5 with a pixie cut hairstyle on her light brown hair. The right side of her nose was pierced and she dressed in the most expensive clothing, always looking to be on the front cover of any magazine that would take her. But everyone liked her because she was cute and really sweet, but she was known on campus for being the teacher's pet.

"My dad and I have come to the conclusion that it must be something in the headache pills I take a night that is affecting my dreams," I signed.

"Oh, that's weird…well how long do you have left on the medication?"

"Today's my last day and I couldn't be more thankful. I'm not the biggest fan of taking medication."

"You wouldn't happen to have any spare pills would you?"

"No Carmen."

"Oh, come on…I would only need one. I want to meet Daniel too. It's not fair that you're the only one who gets to meet him."

"I didn't ask to meet him, Carmen. It just happened, and I'm sorry, but I only have one pill left, and I'm happy to say that I am officially headache free."

"If you're headache-free, then why do you need to take your last pill?"

"Doctors orders."

"Well, I'm happy for you, Grace," she signed.

"I'm happy for me too. Oh, and did I mention that I've been teaching him some sign language. He's actually a really fast learner. Sometimes we only speak in sign language, because he wants to make sure he has the hang of it."

"Your dreams are so real. I mean you're teaching him and he remembers days later when you visit him again. It's so romantic," she sighed as she looked down at her watch. "We better go, or we're going to be late for class."

"Do we really have to go? It's only English class and she's only talking about Alice in Wonderland again...I've already read that story like five times."

Carmen laughed and looped her arm through mine, "Come on."

I took a nap that afternoon when I arrived home from school. I didn't take any of my medicine because it was prescribed to only be taken twice a day, and I always took the first at breakfast and the second after dinner. But I hoped that I would still see Daniel when I closed my eyes during my nap, and thankfully I did.

"My Mom is talking about wanting to take me to a psychiatrist," I told Daniel when I met him on the bench.

"Why? Because you're living half your life in black and white? I suppose that makes sense. She's only worried for you, Grace. Be thankful that you have a mother who cares."

"I am thankful, but I have begun to enjoy my life here, but I enjoy my real life, too. I enjoy my dreams because here I can hear, plus it's like I'm actually living life in a different world. And my parents know that I'm only here because of the pills, and I'm taking my last pill tonight. I might not see you again after tonight."

"Yes, we have discussed that."

"You don't appear to be very heartbroken about it."

He laughed, "Did you want me to be heartbroken? I have been prepared that one day the person I help, will leave me. Just as one day I must leave this place as well."

"Are you scared?"

"Maybe a little, but I have faith that wherever I end up is the place that God wants me to be."

"I pray that you end up somewhere wonderful! Do you think that you'll end up going to a place where you have to help more people?"

"That's what my aunt and uncle think. Where else would I go? I've only been brought up and trained to know this life."

"Yeah. Well, I will miss you Daniel and our talks. You're a really great listener, you know that?"

"Thank you. So are you," he nudged me and smiled.

"Yes well, I like to treat my neighbors the way I want to be treated."

"Yes. That is a good trait to have."

"You know you never answered my question that I asked you last week."

"What question is that?"

"What do you do with your time here, when I'm not here."

"Oh, that. I walk a lot. There's actually a nice trail and pond that I spend a lot of my time at. Would you like to see it?"

I nodded. But as soon as I did, I felt someone nudging my arm. It happened repeatedly until I closed my eyes on Daniel and awoke to see my mother.

My mom woke me up and informed me that Carmen was waiting for me in the living room.

"Hey, are you ready to finish going over Alice in Wonderland?" Carmen signed when I met her.

"Sure, come on in," I signed motioning her to my bedroom.

My bedroom was once used as my place of escape in this house. Now that my whole world was silent, I didn't want to escape from the noise, but to it. Maybe one day someone will walk through my door, scream my name, and I'll hear them. Then this nightmare would finally be over. But since that didn't seem like it was bound to happen anytime soon, I had my dreams. At least for tonight. I finally had a place where I could escape to the noise instead of away from it.

Carmen tapped my arm as she put her book down on my purple zebra print bed sheets. "Do you have any pain reliever? Patricia decided to show up early this month," she signed pointing to her tummy.

"Sure, it's in the medicine cabinet in the kitchen," I signed fully understanding what she was talking about.

She headed towards the kitchen to get her medicine.

But how was I to know that she was going to take my last prescription pill and replace it with an aspirin? How was she to know that my parents and doctor discovered years ago that I have a severe allergic reaction to aspirin? The doctor prohibited me from taking aspirin because it caused me to have stomach pain, nausea, and severe vomiting. She didn't know. I never told her. She only wanted to meet Daniel.

She came back after a few minutes had passed and we began to discuss our homework. I looked at the assignment prompt once more, *Why did the Red Queen want to behead everyone that irked her?* I sighed as I grabbed my computer and began to type out my response. After two hours had passed both Carmen and I had finished our response papers. She left with an unidentifiable smile on her face as I went to join my family for dinner.

"Did you get everything finished?" my mom signed to me across the dinner table.

I nodded as I bit into my spaghetti.

"Did you need me to help you with any of your homework?" my dad signed, "I've read that book a few times myself."

I laughed and shook my head. "No thank you, daddy." My dad didn't read unless he had to, he would rather watch football or re-runs of an old television show.

"Can I read the book now, since you're finished with it?" Benjamin signed.

"Yes sir, you can."

He grinned proudly and took a sip of orange juice from his cup. "Thank you."

Soon enough we had all finished our food and were heading to bed. I had only been in my room for a few minutes before my mom slowly opened my door. "Did you take your last pill?" my mom signed as she made her way towards me.

I nodded as I sighed with relief that it was finally over.

"How are your headaches?"

"Gone. Thankfully."

"I'm happy to hear it. Alright, I'll let you get to sleep. I'll see you in the morning."

She came over and gave me a light kiss on my forehead before leaving the room. I watched as she turned the lights off before I closed my eyes and waited for my dream to awaken me on a bench beside Daniel.

Daniel was waiting for me at the bench as I arrived. I surprised him with a hug that I needed. I knew that this would probably be the last time I would see him again, so I wanted to have the feeling of comfort, warmth, and safety that I knew his hugs would bring. For some odd reason, his hugs helped me to forget about the issues of my own life and they helped to bring clarity into my mind. This world…the world where I spent every night... brought me endless joy. Here I could breathe freely, I could love, and I could enjoy life the way I should be able to.

I released my hold on him and watched as he gave a shocked facial expression. "What was that for?"

"That was for being a good friend to me these past few days and for showing me around your very odd homeland."

"I know that you are going to miss me Grace, but I promise you that you will do fine. You have more strength inside your bones than you know."

"Are you going to miss me as well?"

He seemed to think about it for a second before nodding, "I will. I believe that I have a greater friendship with you than I do with any of my friends here."

"You've never spoken of your friends here before. Where are they? Can I meet them?"

"They are around."

"You keep saying that about everyone I want to meet. Why is that?"

"They will not come out until you are fully whole again and are no longer in the need of an escape. Right now they might as well be as cardboard as those buildings in the distance."

I looked over to where he was pointing and noticed that the

buildings were no longer cardboard as they had been for the past week. They were alive and in vibrant color. I started to wonder what was happening when I suddenly felt that something was wrong. As I slept, a surging pain began to nudge the corners of my mind. I didn't realize what was happening, but I knew I felt wrong somehow.

As if a green light had gone off, people began to come out from the building and houses. The beams from the sun were alive and hot as the clouds in the sky floated by at a normal pace. The grass was no longer gray, but a normal shade of green. Yellow taxi cabs and blue buses suddenly appeared right in front of us. People piled out of the buildings rushing to-and-fro while yelling and talking about things that I could not understand. Cars came out of nowhere and the people that were driving honked at others who were walking in the streets, demanding that they hurry up and move. Dogs chased cats up trees that were now blossoming in full color. Children were running around wildly ignoring their parents and harassing each other. Everything seemed to have shifted from the twentieth century to the twenty-first in a matter of seconds.

"Who are all these people? Where did they all come from?" I asked Daniel.

"I don't know…some of them I know and recognize, but other people I have never seen before in my life. I don't know what is happening. Tell me, is everything around you in color?"

"Yes, and suddenly it's like you're in my world."

"Your world? How can that be possible?"

He looked at me puzzled then said, "Grace, are you okay? You don't look good."

Pain shot through my stomach. "Something is wrong. I feel nauseous."

People suddenly saw Daniel and I on the sidewalk talking and began running towards us like an angry mob yelling, "Off with their heads!"

Daniel and I got off the bench and ran in the opposite direction of the people who wanted to behead us. As we ran I clutched my stomach, only to stop short behind Daniel as he pointed to a bus.

"That bus. That's the bus you were supposed to come into

town on. That's the first time I've seen it since you've arrived. We should get you on it…I think it's headed out of town."

Daniel got the drivers' attention and was able to get him to stop. He stepped aboard and the bus immediately took off.

"Grace, take my hand," Daniel yelled as he reached for me despite the bus's speed.

I reached for it, but before I could fully grasp it, someone grabbed me from behind and started to pull me into the pile of screaming people.

"Grace!" Daniel yelled as the bus picked up speed and drove away.

"Daniel!" I sobbed as I felt fire near my face. Why did I smell fire?

"Down with her!" someone yelled.

"Let's burn her at the stake!" someone else shouted.

It was getting hotter. Who was putting the torch so close to my face? Someone tugged at my arm…stop it! "Stop it! Stop it!"

"Grace! Grace, wake up," I heard someone say in the distance.

I opened my eyes to see my mom in front of me, wiping my face with a cool towel.

"Baby what's wrong? You were yelling in your sleep? Are you okay?" my mom signed.

"I feel sick, my stomach hurts, and I feel nauseous. It's like I had an aspirin or something." My mouth began to feel salty.

"Did you take an aspirin last night?"

"No, no I don't…I only took my prescription."

"Are you sure?"

"I don't–" I stopped signing as I leaned over and vomited onto my brown carpet.

Four Days and Zero Pills Later

"Grace, we have a new student here today who is in need of a dance partner. Do you mind sacrificing your time to be a dancer this week?" my dance teacher signed.

"Sure thing, Mrs. Leanne."

"Good, he's over signing in on the roll sheet. Go over the basics with him and then get started."

I nodded and walked off towards the tall, brown-haired student who was signing the roll sheet.

"Hey Grace, you look good," Carmen called as she briskly passed by me to look for her dance partner.

Carmen and I hadn't talked since the day she switched my pills. She had apologized every day since, I told her I forgave her, but I didn't think it was a good idea to be friends at the moment. She said she understood. I said I hoped she didn't dream about Daniel. She didn't. It serves her right.

I approached the stranger and waited behind him for a second before tapping him on the shoulder. He turned around and the smile I had ready, froze on my face.

"Daniel?" I gasped as he smiled upon noticing me.

"Hello Grace," he signed, "I had hoped this was the school you assist with."

"What are you...how are you...how did you–?"

"I don't know. The bus kept driving and soon enough I was here in this world that you were always talking about. I thought at first that it might be the place that everyone from my home goes, but I quickly found out that I was wrong. I don't know anyone here. So I decided to look for you...and here you are. Are you feeling better?"

I stood flabbergasted at him for a moment. I didn't know what to say. How did he get here? What was he doing here? What did this mean? Was he going to have to go back? Where would he live? Would he have to go to school?

"I know you Grace and I know that you are silently trying to analyze every tiny bit of this situation as we speak."

I looked up at him speechless. I cleared my throat and signed slowly, "Are you not?"

"Oh no, I am. Probably more so than you. But as I've said in the past, God has a reason for everything."

"What's his reasoning behind this?"

"Everyone please grab your partner and begin to start your warm-ups. If you do not have a dance partner please see me or Grace and we will help you to find one or get in line to have one for the next song," Miss Leanne said over the microphone of the ballet studio.

I stood in awe of Daniel for a moment as I watched him look around at all the couples that were starting to warm up. I felt a tap on my shoulder from behind me. I turned to see Carmen looking entranced at Daniel.

"Yes," I signed to her.

"My dance partner, Lucas, has not shown up yet. Would you mind if I shared your dance partner?" she signed not taking her eyes off of Daniel.

I guess I had to thank Carmen in a way, if it wasn't for her switching out my pills, Daniel probably would not be in my world today. Standing beside me wanting to dance, waiting to see what was next in God's plan for his life. But at the same time, Carmen almost killed me because she wanted to see Daniel and didn't care about the consequences of her actions in the long run either. If she were to dance with him, and he were to grow to like her. What would happen to me?

I looked at her about to give a reply when I noticed Lucas walking in from the back door of the studio. I tapped Carmen on the shoulder and pointed her in the direction of Lucas. She pouted slightly before walking off in his direction.

"Shall we begin our warm-ups?" Daniel signed after she had left.

He watched as I sat on the floor and began to stretch, "How long do you think you'll be here?"

"Do you want me to go?"

"No, of course not. I was only wondering. If I'm being honest. ..I'm glad that you're here. I thought that I would never see you again."

"If I'm being honest…so am I. I'm also happy that I found you so easily. Thankfully I remembered one of our many discussions about your ballet studio and the name of it."

I nodded, "So you still believe that this is all a part of God's plan?"

"Yes, I do." He signed as he stood up and offered his hand to me.

"So what happens next?"

"I guess we will have to wait and see."

∾ ∾ ∾

Puzzle

He laid the box beside him, and
placed the pieces on the table before me.

What does it form, I asked?
You will have to wait and see.

Many years started to pass by and I found,
A place for many of the pieces in the puzzle.

When will I see the final picture, I asked?
You will see it when it is time.

Years continue to fly by and I began to see a wedding. I desperately
sought to find the piece that belonged next to mine.

Where is this piece, I asked, I can't find it.
You will find it when it is time. Work on the rest of the puzzle first.

Disappointed, I continued to work on the puzzle. I began to see a
High School, a few jobs, the college I would attend, and a few rare
best friends.

I still can't find the piece that belongs beside mine, I said.
Be patient little one, do not fret, in time it will find you.

How does a puzzle piece find its place in this large puzzle?

Do you know where the missing piece is?
Yes, little one I do.
Why won't you tell me?
Because it is not yet time for you to know.

As I waited I tried to fit many pieces into the spot.
But I never found the perfect fit.

I did get close once or twice,
But close only counts in horseshoes.

Once I found a piece that I thought for certain would fit.
But no matter how hard I tried to force it, it wouldn't stick.

Eventually, I gave up and returned back
to the rest of the puzzle.

Until one day, one day when I returned to work on the puzzle,
I saw a piece that I hadn't noticed before.

It had always been there, but I never thought it would fit. It didn't
look the way I thought it would. But when I tried, it fit.

It fits, Lord! It fits!
The missing piece of the puzzle has been found.

It was never lost, dearest one.
You were only looking in all the wrong places.

One Day

I never see you anymore. You use to appear in my dreams daily, but
now it's been months since I have seen you. Where have you gone?
I prayed last night that you would visit me. But you didn't show.
Where have you gone? Did the time for us end? Me and you. I
knew that it was never meant to be, but the memories still remain. I
will keep them with me forever. Don't forget about me in your new
season of life and love. I hope to see you again, if for only one day.

THE PLAY

"So what part did you get in the play?" Kelly, my best friend, asked.

"I got the lead role!" I replied.

"Really? So did I."

"Did you get the lead role too?" Bridget asked coming over to talk to Kelly and I. "That's weird."

"Did everyone get the lead role?"

"I wonder what the play is about; Mr. Peter refuses to tell anyone about it."

"I know! It's driving me crazy," I said looking over at Mr. Peter.

"Ok class, everyone take a seat so we can talk about the play," Mr. Peter, said aloud to the theater filled with twenty-five students and five hundred empty red seats. "The play that we will be performing is based on a life story...your life story to be more specific. I have written this play myself and you will be under my direction. You have the free will to do as you wish with improvisation and your life choices will be left up to you, but remember that I know the plot, the beginning, middle, and end."

"It sounds great. So when do we get the script?" Kelly asked.

"I will give you one piece of the script at a time. We will be dividing this play into chapters and every day that you come to class I will give you a different line from that chapter."

"Well, that doesn't make any sense? Why don't you just give us the entire script right now?"

"I want you to think of this play as your own personal life story. You don't know what to expect today or tomorrow. You must take life one day at a time or in this case one line at a time. Eventually, you will receive the entire script, just as you will know your life story when you reach the end. If I were to give you the entire story now you would no longer be surprised by the ending. You would know what college you were going to...who you were going to marry... how many kids you were going to have...what career you would take on...the day you would die, and so forth. This way I am leaving the ending opened to your imagination."

"If you already know how the story will end, then that doesn't give us much free will does it?"

"Yes, it does. Just because I know the ending of your story, doesn't mean that you do. You have a choice to make good and bad decisions on a day to day basis. I don't make them for you, you do. I don't help you to study for a test, you do. I don't tell you what to and not to say to your friends and family members, you do. However, I do know how your life will end and what you will do with it. But free will? Yes, that's yours."

"So how long is this play going to last? I mean, if you're only going to give us one line at a time, don't you think it will last past the end of this semester," Kelly asked as she rolled her eyes.

"Yes, I do believe that it will last past the end of the semester. Actually, it will last for the rest of your life until the play comes to an end. That is why I made the play this way."

"This is stupid," Kelly whispered over to me. "Why can't he be a normal teacher and give us the entire script so that we can perform it in front of our junior class like the rest of the high school teachers."

"He's trying to teach us a lesson," I concluded, "and I think it's a great idea. I wish more teachers would teach a class in the perspective of God's eyes. It makes life much more supernatural."

"In a way, but don't you think it's a waste of time. I mean he knows how the play will end, but we won't. It doesn't make any sense," Bridget responded.

"Are we going to perform this to our junior class?" Matt asked from the front row.

"Actually Matt we will. We will perform in December every line that we have covered," Mr. Peter said grinning.

"This is stupid, it's unprofessional. I knew I should've taken art," Kelly leaned over to say to me and Bridget.

"I like the idea. In fact...Mr. Peter," I said raising my hand.

"Yes?"

"I think this play is an excellent idea, and I'm ready to take on my part in your play. You're the director. You know better than anyone what you are doing. If we all wrote our own life stories the play would be a complete and total disaster. Give us the order and the life stories that you want us to have, because you know what best fits our personality. I'm ready to be an actress in your story. Tell me what to do."

"Alright, anyone else?"

"Wait, is that why we all got the lead part in the play?" Jake, a boy in the back of the theater asked.

"Yes, you all have the leading role in your own life. Everyone in this theater right now is equally important, whether you know it or not."

"This is so weird," a voice said in the back of the theater.

"I thought this class was supposed to be an easy A?" a girl's voice asked aloud.

"Your grade completely depends on you, your actions, and the choices you make," Mr. Peter stated.

"So," I asked, "when do we start?"

Birds

Listen to the birds as they sing their perfect melody.
Birds have it so easy.

Watch the birds as they fly into the sunset.
Never looking behind them. They keep moving forward.

They don't try to please anyone in particular.
They are birds. Only doing as God instructed.

Singing their sweet tunes and not feeling burdened
by the necessities and pressures of life.

I wish I was a bird just for a day.
To sing as they do. Then fly away.

Junior Year

I was drawn to him as he was to me. Both in different ways. I
wanted to teach him, to help him with his marching. He wanted to
be with me, to have me. There was only one thing on his mind. I
rejected him. He didn't take no for an answer. And as any baby does,
he went crying to his father. "Why won't you date my son?" his
father asked. "Do you think you're too good for him?" he wanted
to know. My brother noticed me crying as I ran away and climbed in
my father's car to go home. My dad saw me cry. My dad never felt
fear as I had. He only implanted fear. Especially into anyone who
hurt his family. He made sure I was safe, secure, protected. I never
heard from that young boy ever again.

Receiving Peace

Over the past nine years, I have counseled many people with different problems, and have found that all are after the same thing: peace. Peace of mind and the ability to move on with their life. Some of the problems that I hear are minor and can be fixed with time and perspective, like failing out of college or breaking up with a longtime lover. Others are more severe, for instance finding out a spouse is cheating after years of marriage or an unexpected divorce. The minor problems involve me doing a lot of note-taking and nodding my head from time to time while the more severe cases can take hours of intense therapy. One client…my most recent, had a story unlike any other that I had heard before. Her name was Annie, and her request overwhelmed me. She didn't want peace of mind about the memories she had made over the years, she wanted to completely forget them. She wanted her memories erased. All of them.

"Hello Annie, nice to see you again," I said coming from behind my desk to shake her hand.

"Hello, Dr. Bloom, nice to see you as well," Annie said taking my hand.

"If you will take a seat we can begin," I said gesturing to the chaise lounge as I sat opposite her.

"Did you think over my proposal? Have you decided if this is the best decision for you?"

"I have thought about it, and I've decided that I want to do this."

"You're sure? I said looking at her intensely, "because you know that once its over-"

"Yes, I'm sure," Annie interrupted. I've considered the outcome of my decision and I've decided that this is the best thing for me."

Three years ago a machine was created called the Mem-E-Mac. My psychiatric team and I were given the machine to try to see if it would help to prosper or reduce the amount of clients and money that was being brought into our offices. The machine is very simple to explain, it erases memories. Yes, the very memories that people want to forget so that they can move on with their lives can be erased out of their head. The catch is the person can only use it once.

We decided as a psychiatric team to introduce the machine to anyone with a severe problem, especially if it seemed that they were on the verge of committing suicide.

"Do you remember what we discussed last week Annie?"

"About the machine? Yes I remember."

"You understand that the way the machine works is it removes the memories from one's brain whether they are good or bad. The way the machine works is that it has the ability to remove the memories located in your prefrontal cortex, by concentrating on the memory you want erased the machine has easy access to what you want erased and it will be cleared from your memory in less than thirty minutes."

The first client that was offered the use of the machine came into my friend Rupert's office crying every day. She had been raped earlier that year by her cousin twice a week for a month when she was fifteen. Her parents were on their twenty-five year honeymoon and had placed her aunt along with her twenty-three year old son in charge of watching her while they were out of town. Her cousin threatened her daily not to tell anyone what was happening between them. It was during summer and school was out. He watched her relentlessly, and threatened to kill her if she told anyone. She had no contact with the outside world except what he would allow. Her aunt worked twelve hour shifts so she had no one in whom to confide. Two months after her parents had returned home, she came forward with the news. Her cousin was sent to prison for ten years and her mom sent her to Rupert. The Mem-E-Mac helped her remarkably. She was finally able to move on with her life, without the remembrance of her cousin raping her floating around in the back of her brain. The tears were behind her.

"I have agreed to those terms."

"But what I want to remind you Annie, is that you asked for not one memory to be erased, but all of your memories to be erased. I know you already know this information, but I must repeat it as a formality. Are you certain of your decision?"

I saw her look off in the distance. Her gaze fell to the window to my right. The tree branches swayed in the wind, hitting the window every so often, because they had no way of controlling themselves. I looked back over at Annie and began to consider the thoughts floating around in her head. She didn't want to be ruled by her past life and memories any longer. She wanted a fresh start…a clean slate.

"Yes, I'm sure. I don't see any other option. It's either getting my memories erased or jumping off the highest bridge I can find, and I'm afraid of heights. That's why I was referred here," she said answering my question.

There were other successful stories that were associated with the Mem-E-Mac. Some of the people who had used the machine had lost their loved ones due to various reasons, some had accidentally killed another person due to a car accident, and some had watched their loved ones die in their arms, while others had experienced their spouse having an affair with a friend, family member, or stranger. The problem with having your memories erased is that you can't recall the mistakes you've made in the past. Some of the clients I've had have moved on with their lives satisfied and full of joy and peace. Others have moved on thinking that they are making a change in their life, when really they begin making the same mistakes they made before.

I never agreed with the invention of the Mem-E-Mac, my view on the machine was different from that of my colleagues. Instead of helping our clients to put their faith in Jesus the only one who can truly give them peace, they encourage our clients to find the easy way out by having their memories erased, which does not help them to learn from their memories and mistakes. They want to put their faith in a man-made machine that could fail them at any moment.

"Annie, I have you scheduled to go in the day after tomorrow, is that correct?"

"Yes," she said tearing her eyes away from the window and back to me, "that is correct."

"Very good." I glanced at my Rolex, "We still have forty minutes left. Why don't you tell me the memory that you want to forget."

"I never saw it coming," she said holding her gaze on me, "I'd do anything to re-live that day and change what took place."

"Take your time, Annie," I said placing my pen on my notepad and gesturing for her to continue.

Her story started off as it always did, with her and her best friend Claire getting a cup of coffee from their favorite coffee shop, Pour N' Go.

"What did you publisher say?" Claire had asked as they fixed their coffee.

"I'll have to wait about a week or two for my story to get read. Apparently his desk is already piled up with other author's stories," Annie said taking a sip of her coffee.

"I told you, you should've went to my publisher he loves to work with starting authors like me and you…we're still starting. Two books a piece for the both of us, we're almost there. Antonio is the best; he always gets to my stories in four days or less."

"That could have something to do with you—"

"Hey! Don't judge me! I do what I have to do, to get the job done. You should do the same."

"I will, but I prefer to do it the right way. Not…that way."

"You're such a goody two shoes," Claire said swishing around a mouthful coffee.

"Maybe, but I'll be the one known as a respected author and writer. What will you be known as?"

"Who cares? I'll have my book published faster and that's all that matters."

""Faster" is not always better Claire."

"Whatever, Annie."

After Annie finishes this part of her story she looks off at the window once again. She tells me that they walked around the block until they had finished their coffee. The sun had already begun to go down outside because of the fairly recent time change.

"You ready to head back?" Annie had asked.

"Sure. My house or yours?"

"Yours, I guess. I really don't want to go back to mine at the moment. My mom is still hounding me to get another place."

"You should've kept the house, Annie."

"Why? So the memories of David can flood back through my head every time I walk through the door. No thanks."

"Have you started to get rid of any of his stuff yet?"

"Sort of, my mom and dad are helping out a lot. They're getting tired of it cluttering up the garage."

"Are you keeping anything?"

"His firefighter uniform, there's so many good memories."

"Like playing dress up?"

"He had loved seeing me in his uniform, it's the last piece I have of him…man I miss him," Annie had said letting out a corner smile.

"I know you do."

"There's my car," Annie said. They'd walked three blocks away from the coffee shop.

Annie took her gaze off the window and onto her hands lying in her lap as she continued slowly with her story.

"Soon we got into the car, me in the driver's seat and Claire in the passengers. I started the car and pulled out. Do I really need to continue? We both know how it ends," Annie asked looking down at her hands instead of up at me.

"Please do, Annie."

She sighed placing her left hand over the front of her face, balancing her left elbow on her left thigh. After three minutes she continued.

"I can't believe he's already been gone for seven months."

"Seven months and one week Thursday."

"Annie…"

"I know…he died trying to save another's. My dad is constantly reminding me."

"He's right, you know."

"I know."

At this Annie stopped her story once more, she removed her hand from her face and looked me in the eye saying, "Then it happened, we were stopped at a red light. When it turned green I got off my brake and pressed on the gas and as I eased forward to go through the light some…IDIOT thought he could make the yellow light that he had already…"

"It's okay Annie you can stop."

"He hit her side! That stupid dumb—"

"Ann—"

"She was able to barely say my name before breathing her last breath."

"Anni—"

"I wanted her with me in the ambulance, but no they said she's already gone. But I refused to believe them. Even when they pulled her out and covered her body with a blanket, even when they closed the door to the back of the ambulance leaving her by herself on that cement road! Even when my parents came to the hospital and told me what everyone else already had, even when I saw her being slowly put into the ground a week later at a service that I completely cried through, even when—"

"I know, Annie," I said finally being able to finish a sentence.

"It's not fair! Why Claire…why David? Why must their lives be taken while I'm left to live my life alone?" Annie yelled as tears started to stream down her face.

"Annie, I know that you are upset, but I want you to do something for me can you do that?" I asked softly as I grabbed a few of the tissues that I always had in a box off my desk and handed them to her.

I watched as Annie slowly wiped her tears away, regained her composure and balled her used tissue up in her right hand, "What do you want me to do?"

"I want you to think of one good memory, one that you've had in the past that you wouldn't want erased." I paused to allow her to think about what I'd said. "Do you have one in mind?"

"There isn't a single good memory that remains with me. Claire and David were apart of all my good memories. The ones that were good at one point no longer have the same appeal on me as they once did."

"Annie…think hard, what about your parents?" I asked scribbling something down on my notepad.

"I thought you were supposed to help me get rid of my memories? Not help me hold onto them. Wouldn't you want to be relieved of the memories that kept you up crying at night, if you could?"

"Let me tell you a story Annie." I watched her get comfortable in her chair before I continued, "When I was a junior in high school I caught my girlfriend cheating on me with my best friend. I knew that she had been acting strange around me for a while, but I didn't think anything of it because we loved each other. Well, one early morning I showed up to the Band Hall to get some extra practicing in on my Tuba and I caught the two of them together. The details that follow are not important. What is important is what I tried to do after I saw what I saw."

"Which was…?"

"After two months of trying to get over her and not succeeding, I tried to commit suicide. Haley and I had been together for five years, I felt that my life was over…that I would never again find someone that I could love anywhere near as much as I loved her. So I decided to end it, and put it all behind me."

"So what happened, because it's pretty obvious that you didn't end your life?"

"That's because God stepped in the second I grabbed my dad's revolver from his desk office. I held the gun up to my head and pulled the trigger. Not thinking for one second about the people that I'd be hurting if I left the Earth forever, not about my family, friends, my future career, anything. I was thinking only in the present moment…all I wanted was to end the pain that was beginning to well up inside of me and take over my life. But every time I pulled the trigger, nothing happened. You see my dad had removed the barrel from the gun, because he was out of town and didn't want to leave the gun in his desk drawer fully loaded."

"That's when God stepped in?"

"Soon after that, yes. I ran back into my dad's office looking everywhere for a bullet. All I needed was one. That's when I heard the Lord's voice saying, "Who are you to end the life I have given to you?" I knelt to the ground as I began to cry and scream for the lord to help me. That night I placed my life into his hands, I placed the gun back in my dad's drawer and I haven't touched it since. I believe that God has given us memories and the strength to handle them for a reason. He won't place us into any situation that we can't handle. My memories have made me the man I am today. Memories are meant to strengthen us. Yes, there are some that tear you down, but in the end they make you strong. If you trust and give that burden to Jesus he will share the load with you and you won't be weighed down with the sadness and heartache anymore. That's why God allowed for Jesus to be our Savior and not the machine."

"Isn't there a memory you would want to erase?"

"No. There are times I wish I could change the past, but as far as getting rid of a certain memory altogether, I don't think that I would be able to live knowing that I'm missing a part of me. But this isn't about me, Annie, it's about you. Are you ready to do this?"

She seemed to think about her answer for a second or two before answering. She looked at me and smiled half-heartedly as a tear coursed down her cheek. "I am."

"Okay. Then Annie I will see you back here in two days," I said getting out of my chair.

"How do I get to that place?" Annie asked as she remained in her chair looking at me with empty eyes. "Where I can accept the bad and learn to look forward to life with a smile?"

"I believe in my savior, I have faith that he will bless me with a new day tomorrow, that I can start fresh on everything that has gone wrong."

"That's what I want," she said with a sob.

"You want what, Annie?"

"Peace."

I sighed with a smile and glanced down at my watch once more. My next client wouldn't arrive for another thirty minutes.

"Peace is not something that comes from a machine, Annie. It's something that comes from accepting Christ as your lord and savior…the ruler of your life."

"How does that work, if not by a machine?"

I sat back down in my seat and placed my notepad on my desk behind me and picked up my brown bible that lay beside it, "Annie, I want to introduce you to a friend of mine."

Ghost of a Memory

So many memories are embedded into one season.
Why can one season, the heat, the smell, the feeling in
the air bring back all of those memories.
It used to happen only when Summer came, but not anymore.
Now it comes with Winter too.

Now he comes. Well, his ghost comes. And it never leaves me alone.

He's sneaky like Jack Frost, Santa Clause, and the Tooth Fairy.
You never see him, but you know that he's there.
He always remembers to leave behind a clue.
Something to let you know that he was there.
But he doesn't leave behind frost on your car,
presents under the tree, or even a dollar under your pillow.

No, he's different from them in that area.
He leaves behind hints of memories, thoughts, feelings, emotions.
Memories I thought I had forgotten.
Feelings that should have been buried with him.
I know he will never come back to me, but I still feel him at times.
Those random times when the heat of Summer brushes my cheek.
Or the iciness of Winter reminds me of football games and bonfires.
He makes certain that I can never forget about him.

It sucks being stuck with his ghost. It never leaves me alone.

Every once in a while, I see him too.
He likes to drop into my dreams from time to time to say hi.
I like it when he does that. That way I can never forget his face.
His touch, his smile, his gaze. Everything that I loved about him
and more are always a part of my dreams.
When he drops by in my dreams I don't care. I want him to stay.
Because it feels like he's there. It feels as if anything can happen.
But then I wake and I know that nothing ever will.

It sucks being stuck with his ghost. It never leaves me alone.

Out Loud

She jokes about it all the time.
She thinks it's funny. Planning the future for you and me.
It keeps her entertained. Or maybe she really does have hope for us.
Honestly, I hate it when she does it.
Talk about the future, that is.

I wish there could be a future between me and you.
I've always wanted there to be one. But it's too late now.
You're gone and I'm doing my own thing here.
Plus, you never wanted to be with me anyway.

At least, not out loud.

Why didn't you ever say what your feelings were for me?
Why didn't you ever stand up for me, for us, when it came to your
friends? I guess it doesn't matter now.
Time has left us and there's no way we can turn the clock back.
Not that I'd want to. I liked the past and history that we shared.

It's special to me. I wouldn't want to change it for the world.
It always warms my heart when I think about us. You and me.
What could or might have been. But even more so, I love what we had.
No it wasn't the romance that you see on TV shows, in movies, or
even find in books.
What we had was a give and take relationship.
Ross and Rachel. That's what we were.

You know what I love most about Ross and Rachel.
That after nine years of denying their feelings for one another.
They finally got together.
That could be us. I wish that was us. But I know that it never will be.
Because you're gone and I'm here.
You never had the courage to tell anyone how you felt about me.

At least, not out loud.

What's Your Number?

"I think I only want to have two kids when I get older," my sister said as she watched my mom rock our baby cousin to sleep one afternoon, "one boy and one girl."

"I want three," I said, "I want the same amount that Mommy had."

"I only had three children because I had to have a cesarean section with each of you. And my doctor advised against me having any more children. More than three cesearean sections could have caused something fatal to happen to me or the baby. My desire was to have five children, but it was not meant for me to have more than what I was blessed with," my mom said.

"You should have tried for another, you wouldn't have died. God wouldn't have allowed it."

"I suppose that I was meant to only have three children for a reason, plus it will work out in the end. I'm sure I will have lots of grandkids."

"Yes, you're going to have," I paused for a second to do the math, "seven!"

"Well, hopefully, I will have a lot more than that. I want at least twenty grandkids."

"Do you have some hidden children somewhere we don't know about?" my sister asked sarcastically.

"It's okay Mommy, I'm going to have nine children so that'll help you reach your number," my five-year-old brother chimed in.

"Nine! Why would you want nine?" I asked.

"So that one can play with me, one can do my chores, one can cook for me, and one can clean my bedroom…" he listed off.

My mom came from a family of seven children and explained that although they had their share of hard times, she loved being a part of a large family. "Children are important. Not just for society has a whole, but because they are a part of the future generation. You should want as many children as the Lord blesses you with. It is through your children that change will happen in the world." She went on to explain that the bible describes children as arrows in the hands of a warrior. They have to be shaped and molded lovingly and diligently to be able to "hit the mark" when the time comes. She made it clear to us that children were not burdens, but blessings that God gives to parents to help make a change in the world. "I'm not saying that one child can't make a change, but say for instance if you had five," she told us, "there is a greater chance for effective change. Children are like arrows in your quiver. The more you have…the greater chance that you will hit your mark. Once you send them out of your hand, how you have prepared them beforehand, will decide the change they will make in the world."

"What in the world is a qu-ver?" I had asked as my nine-year-old brain tried to comprehend the word.

"Think about what I have told you," my mom reiterated. "As you get older, maybe you will decide that two or three children will be too few for you." I thought about that conversation with my mom many times. My sister and I use to think that we would never want to have that many children, but sure enough, as the years flew by we changed our numbers.

It wasn't until we were in our late teens to early twenties that we changed our number. My sister changed hers from two to four, but only after getting married and having her first child. My brother changed his from a made-up nine to five, with a slight influence from me and my mom. But mine was the biggest leap of all.

When I turned thirteen I began working in the children's ministry at my church. Although I was still a child myself, I had a desire to serve, encourage, and influence the younger children around me. I enjoyed teaching the younger children to sing songs, play games, and pray. When I was sixteen I got my first babysitting job and I came to realize that I really enjoyed taking care of and spending time with smaller children. I was in charge of a three-month-old baby and a three-year-old child, for several hours and a few days at a time. I quickly began to realize that I had a natural instinct when it came to taking care of children. My mom and others told me that I had a way of loving and caring for children that automatically drew them to me. My mom called it, a motherly instinct. Needless to say, my parents were not surprised when I announced to them one day that I no longer wanted three children, but I was hoping that I would be able to have seven. I informed them that I wanted to have five of my own, adopt two, and if the Lord wanted to bless me with more, then so be it.

Although I would be very glad to be able to have seven children, there are many people who think this number is going a little overboard. Whenever anyone asks me how many kids I intend to have, I reply that I want seven. This reply is usually followed by a shocked look and stunned silence. Many times I receive a disgusted expression or a strange look in return.

"Why would you want to have seven kids?" most people ask.

"You'll never have any time for yourself or your husband," others say.

"If you can't afford them, you'll become a hobo and live under a bridge with only the fish that you catch on occasion for food. Why would you do that to yourself?" A random stranger asked me.

But my favorite by far is, "Oh honey, you'll never get your figure back."

It is as if the only things that are important in life are the way you look, how much free time you have on your hands, and how much money you hold in the bank. My reply to all of these questions are, "I love kids and I'm ready to have a large family of my own…I never have time for myself anyway, with school and work. What is free time anyway?…Who says that having seven children will make me a hobo and if it does, I don't mind living off the land, it'll teach my children to be strong and how to fend for themselves…I don't have much of a figure anyway, so that's fine…plus with seven children, I'll be so busy running and chasing after them that I'll probably lose and drop pounds unintentionally and end up smaller than I am now, so it all works out for the best." The adventures that come with having children are a part of life. Why wouldn't I want to embrace that?

After getting so much push back from inquiring people, I decided to do a little research. I found out that the fertility rate has begun to slowly decrease in the United States. In 2013 the average fertility rate was 2.06. A year earlier than that in 2012, the average amount of births was 63 per 1000 women compared to the 127 births per 1000 women that were recorded in 1909. So why has our number decreased in the last 100 years? If we compare a country like Uganda to the United States, they had a 6.06 fertility rate in 2013, while Niger had a 7.03. According to statistics, the United Kingdom has a greater percentage of children (three or more per household) than three-quarters of the European Union which includes Germany, Greece, Spain, and Poland. Data shows that the poorest places on earth have the highest numbers of families with children. So why are Americans having fewer children now than they did in the past? Part of the reason this is happening is because there are less farming communities.

While speaking to my Grandpa, he told me that when he was growing up, people often had five or more children because they usually owned several acres of farmland and needed the extra hands. There were more mouths to feed, but because they lived off the land it usually provided food for them. In our current day, there are few people who have farms or several acres of land to farm so therefore most people do not want many children. "Why have a large number of children, when they can't work and help to feed themselves?" He said. He calls it the "shrinking of the American family." He told me that it appears that every generation has less and less children. "Other nations are having more children, while Americans keep having less."

Is there a chance that people will decide once again to have large families? Well, let's take my grandma for example. My grandma is the proud mother of seven children and the grandmother of nine. When I asked if she would have the same amount of children all over again, her answer was a resounding "No".

"If I had to do it all over again, I wouldn't go past two."

"Why?"

"Because then I would not have had to sacrifice as much time and energy raising children as I did. I would have had more time to myself, and I would not have had children living at home so long. When you have several children there are times that you struggle for money and paying the bills. With fewer children, I would have had less to worry about and your grandpa and I would have been able to travel more and had more finances for our older years. Yeah, if I had to do it again, I would definitely stop at two. Why? How many are you planning to have?"

"Seven."

"You'll change your mind after you have your first. Trust me."

"But if I only have two…then they'll grow up too fast and leave the house after college and then it will only be me and my husband left in the house…bored. What if they don't get along with one another? At least if I had more than two there is a larger possibility that they will each have a friend and confidant around. What if I end up having two girls? Then I'll never know what it's like to have a son…or what if I have two boys? Then if I only have two kids, then I can't have my own miniature school or have my really large one story home, because I don't need a large one story home if I only have two kids. What if they both die in their teens and I'm not able to have any more children? Then there will be no one left to carry on the family name or inherit everything in our home, so then I'll have to give it all to my sister or brother… and that's no fun. Plus if I have seven kids, then there will be no need for babysitters in the house, and when it comes to dating we will have plenty of chaperones to keep watch."

My grandma looked at me strangely after I had finished, "Like I said, you'll change your mind."

"I don't think so. I'm looking forward to my seven children or more if that's what God allows."

That is the viewpoint that the majority of Americans hold. Most couples are postponing marriage and children until they are stable financially and this could mean waiting ten to fifteen years. When they do decide to have a family, one to two children are the desired number. They want more time and money to themselves. There are now more households with dogs than children. Why, because as my grandma stated, "Kids are too expensive and they take up too much time. I could be using that money and extra time for myself."

Psalm 127:3-5 reads: "Behold, children are a heritage from the Lord, the fruit of the womb a reward. Like arrows in the hand of a warrior are the children of one's youth. Blessed is the man who fills his quiver with them! He shall not be put to shame when he speaks with his enemies in the gate." These verses are always my mom's go-to reference whenever she is talking to anyone about the number of children they want to have.

I once had a co-worker who miscarried three babies during the time when she and her husband were trying to have children. After finally deciding on adoption, her physician tried one last medical procedure and she conceived a beautiful baby boy. Their story has been a blessing to several women who have tried to conceive and failed and showing them that through their struggle there is always hope. She, however, was not impacted in the same way as I believe I would have been. Although she lost three babies before she was finally blessed with her son, she is happy with her one child. She has said that she may decide in the near future to try for one more, but currently, she and her husband are satisfied with the family they now have. Even though I know that every one must decide their own destiny, it makes me wonder why they went through all of that pain, trial and suffering for one quiver.

It takes a lot of commitment, dedication, strength, and

patience to have children, whether you decide to have one or seven. It is only God that will ultimately provide no matter how many children you decide is right for you. God allows each child to come into the world and they are his children. I may have a certain number, but only God knows the outcome.

Now when people ask me how many children I intend to have my answer is, "I plan to have seven. I want to have five and adopt two unless God says otherwise because I'm raising them for the Lord. They are God's children as well as my own. I don't care what the world thinks of me as I drive around in my big yellow bus and have to call roll every time we get on and off because that's what I want and hopefully what God allows for my life. I want as many quivers in my bow as I can possibly have."

Daughter to Mother

When I was an infant, you were my nurturer.
You sustained and provided for me,
while your loving arms kept me safe.
You were the mother who cared for me.

When I became old enough I went off to kindergarten,
you dressed and taught me to stand strong.
No matter the difficulty.
You served as both my teacher and guide.

When I became a teenager and thought that I knew it all,
you explained that life was not always as it seemed and no one
had the monopoly on knowledge. You continued to see me
through my hard times as you prayed for me.

When I became a young woman,
you taught me how to be a proper young lady
although I assured you they no longer existed.
You were the mother that instructed and encouraged me.

When I became a wife I thought I understood you at last,
you told me how proud you were to have me as your daughter.
As tears slid gently down your cheeks, you wanted to hold on,
but it was time to let me go.

When I birthed my first child,
I felt lost and confused about the new life in my arms.
But you guided me through and let me know you had been there too.
You became the mother who was a both a listener and friend.

Though our relationship has changed with the passing of years,
You have always been there, as a friend.
And you will always remain my mother.

Growing Up

The best part about aging is the memories
that come with it. The experiences, that have
been had and the laughs and smiles that allow
us to stay young.

The marriages that come when friends find their
long sought after love and the heartbreak that
follows when a loved one leaves us.

I never thought I'd reach this moment to look back
and be thankful for everything and everybody who
who I have had the chance to share my life with.

Each moment is more special than the last, because
I am still alive to embrace it.

Every once in a while, I am reminded of him,
Christmas and spring breaks always reveal
a memory that I have secretly kept locked away.

Then I begin to have lingering thoughts about the
what could have been.' But I wipe my tears and keep moving
forward because that's all a part of growing up.

One Righteous Person

The Heart of Man

The king banged his fist on the nightstand. "Ignorant and selfish people. Every one of them. Why can't there be one? Just one decent person, in the entirety of my kingdom," King Jeremiah asked his wife.

She listened to him rant while semi-distracted by the servant girl who, at the queen's command, was in the process of snuffing out the candles along the wall.

"Well?" he asked insistently.

"Remember my husband," Queen Gabriella said smiling, "you decided that it was important to walk among the people as a commoner. You were the one who wanted to know the lives and manner of your people. What did you expect?"

"Well, now I know and I am shamed by what I see. When did these servants…my subjects, the people of my land begin to behave so terribly?" the king demanded.

The queen looked at him bemused, "They did not just begin to carry these traits and faults, my dear. It has always been so. It has always been in the heart of man, has it not? Since the beginning of time. Man cannot help himself. Sin abides in each creature because of the fall, you know this as much as anyone. It is no wonder that God destroyed everyone but Noah and his family in the great flood as the scriptures tell us. Why did he begin again with Noah? He wanted a fresh start, a new people. But where did that lead? Sin is fixed in the heart of man my beloved. Does not the story of Adam and Eve clearly tell us this?"

"Yes dear, you speak truth but," he took a seat on his burgundy couch, a color of his wife's choosing a few months ago, "why can't I find one person in my entire kingdom? When did it get so wicked?"

"Why are you so sure that it hasn't always been this wicked? When was it last that you spent time with the people before now?"

He considered and thought about her question for a long while. She continued, "I know you're worried about what will happen when Joseph takes over the kingdom, but-"

"Out of the question! No son of mine will take over such an unruly kingdom. I can hardly do so myself now, after everything I've seen."

She looked at him sharply, "Shall you live forever? What do you intend to do?"

"I'm not sure how, but I intend to find an answer that will benefit not just the people, but the entire kingdom."

He got off of his couch and paced back and forth. He suddenly snapped his fingers and spoke to the young servant girl who was slowly snuffing out each candle. "Don't put out that last light. Bring me a lamp and my bible. I have some reading to do."

Destroying the Kingdom

"I will do it!" King Jeremiah proclaimed.

"What gives you the right?" Queen Gabriella asked.

"Right? I have every right! I am king!"

"I am queen and I believe that such a drastic decision is preposterous!"

Joseph sat silently looking back and forth at his parents at the opposite end of the table as they continued to discuss and argue over the matter at hand. Joseph was a noble young man. His curly black hair and olive complexion stood out in stark contrast to his gray-green eyes. He stood well over six feet in height and his mother had begun to say that he was no longer a boy, but had grown into a handsome young man. He had just turned seventeen and often thought about what the kingdom would be like when he became king. He believed that his father was a great king and truly loved his people, but there were times that he was rash. This was one of those times. He did not want to see the kingdom destroyed and everything around him that he had come to know and love come to an end. He barely heard the footsteps of his younger sister approaching from behind him.

"What are they going on about?" Josephine whispered taking her place at the dining table beside her brother.

Josephine was fourteen years old with a strong resemblance to her father, however, her brown eyes and fair complexion she had inherited from her mother. Her thick hair was braided in a crown about her heads accented with a wreath of small pink flowers.

Joseph turned his attention towards his sister and admired her ladies' maid handiwork. He greeted her with a welcoming smile before whispering, "Father plans to destroy every person in the kingdom. He says that we need a fresh start and that there is not one righteous person in the city. He does not want to rule or be associated with a kingdom that is ruthless, selfish, unrighteous, and greedy."

"He can't do that!" Josephine spoke up forgetting to whisper.

"Apparently he can," Joseph remarked, "he's the king."

"What about our children? How will they ever get married if we destroy everyone?" the queen asked her husband.

"There are other kingdoms. Kingdoms that have far finer people than those we have here. They shall be able to find a fit wife and husband among them. Do not trouble my dear Gabriella. We will search everywhere until we find someone well suited for them."

"You believe that the other kingdoms are better off than ours. That the people there are more righteous than the ones here?"

The king remained speechless but bit into his biscuit as he watched his wife let out a long sigh before noticing that her children were seated in their place at the far end of the dining table.

"Good morning children."

They both nodded and smiled in reply. The dining hall was quiet for a long moment until Josephine broke the silence.

"Father, do you really intend to kill everyone in the kingdom?"

"After reading the scriptures last night, yes Josephine I do believe that that is the best decision for my kingdom. The only ones that shall remain are those in the royal household." Josephine's father responded.

"But don't you think the people deserve another chance to redeem themselves."

"It wouldn't help. Every last one of them out there are selfish, greedy, and only think of themselves. I refuse to rule over such barbaric people."

"You don't think there is one person out there that is different from the rest."

"Not that I have seen Josephine and…I am sorry but I have made up my mind."

King Jeremiah summoned the servant and stood up from his chair. "I have spoken to my royal advisors and though they may disagree, my decision shall go into effect at the end of the week."

The king turned around, whispered to the servant and began to walk towards the door.

Everyone remained speechless. Queen Gabriella shook her head in response as tears began to well up in her eyes. She knew her husband was upset, but not even she would have imagined this.

Joseph ate his breakfast in silence. Maybe if he talked to his father, reasoned with him, he would change his mind. He knew his father could be headstrong. But how could he think to kill everyone in the kingdom? What about the army? What if they were attacked? Who would defend them? Maybe this was a test. A test for them all.

Josephine began to think of a way to fix this problem. How on Earth could she stop her father from making such a rash decision? Her father was the king without a doubt, but what sort of king would he be without a kingdom to rule. She had to do something...but what? She glanced at her mother. She was clearly shaken. "It will be okay mother. I promise."

"Father," Josephine asked suddenly, "would you spare the lives of your citizens if you found fifty righteous people?"

The king thought back to the verses he'd read the night before when Abraham asked the same question of God. He stopped walking and turned around to face his daughter. The king smiled softly and nodded his head, "If I found fifty righteous people I would spare the lives of my kingdom. At least then I would know that there was hope."

Josephine nodded as her father again began to walk towards the door. "Would you spare the lives of your citizens if you found twenty righteous people?"

He stopped, turned again to face her and nodded, "Yes if twenty were found. I would spare the lives of everyone.

The king turned once more and started to make his way towards the door that led to the drawing room.

"Father," Josephine spoke up as she rose from her chair. "Would you spare the lives of your people, if you were to find only one righteous person?"

The king did not turn but stopped in his tracks and left his right hand on the knob that led to the drawing room. He seemed to think over his daughter's question for a moment, before letting out a long slow breath.

He finally turned to face his daughter and said quietly, "If we were to find one righteous person in my entire kingdom. I would spare the lives of everyone, for even with that one person, hope can blossom."

As he turned away he heard his daughter say, "Then I shall go into the kingdom dressed up as a beggar as you once did yourself, and see for myself if I cannot find one righteous person."

With that everyone looked up at Josephine then turned their attention to the king, who had taken his hand off the door knob and was making his way back to the table.

The Challenge

"I don't like this one bit. Even less than when you went out and pretended to be a commoner for a week," Queen Gabriella said to her husband as she watched her son and daughter put on the finishing touches of their beggar garments.

"We will be fine mother," Joseph stated, "We will be back no later than eight o'clock, each night during this three day period and I will always be with Josephine, every step of the way."

"We will be fine mother. Don't worry. Joseph will let no harm befall me. Besides," Josephine said squeezing her mother's hand, "I've always loved a good challenge."

"Don't be too disappointed Josephine, when the challenge you have taken upon yourself fails," King Jeremiah said sternly.

"I have faith father. I believe that I will find that person. But what will you do when I find that one person?"

"You mean besides save the lives of all my people?" he responded.

"Yes, father what will you do?" Joseph asked curiously.

"First find that one righteous person and then I will decide what to do."

"Be sure that you do father," replied Josephine.

He smiled down at his strong and wise fourteen-year-old daughter and gave her a quick kiss on the forehead then watched as Lucas, the door guard, opened the front door and ushered both of them out into the city.

• • •

Joseph and his sister walked for miles going further into the city. They approached several strangers, both noble men and women and the common people to ask for food, money, or clothing. The answer remained the same no matter whom they approached. "We only have enough for our own family," or "You are a young enough, make an earnest living for yourself," or "Why don't you put the girl to work for you. She could help you earn a day's wage if you know what I mean."

Joseph admired his sister's courage, strength, and

determination to prove their father wrong. They had always been close. His mother had wished for several children, but due to unknown reasons was unable to bear more. She was his only sibling and he had a dogged determination to protect her at all cost, but sometimes that was hard to do. His sister was strong-willed just like his father and never took no for an answer. If presented with a challenge, she had to prove that she could conquer and overcome it. He only hoped she had not gone too far this time.

They had been away from home for six hours before Josephine saw an old family friend. Lord Henry was one of her favorite people. Whenever he came to visit her mother and father, he always had a present for her and a pocket full of hard candy for her after dinner. Her father told her that he was well traveled and often visited the farthest reaches of the world.

"Look, Joseph, it's Lord Henry. He is sure to give assist if we ask," Josephine stated.

"Let me go to him," Joseph declared. "He will not take kindly to a beggar girl approaching him."

As Joseph approached Lord Henry she noticed him visibly stoop lower as not to reveal his true height. Wrapping her cloak tight around her body to shield her face, Josephine stayed close by her brother. Her maidservant, Hester, had done a great job of disguising her and her brother from passer-byers, but if one were to look to closely, it was possible that they could be found out.

"Excuse me, sir," Joseph said to Lord Henry as he approached him.

"Yes, what is it? I'm in a hurry."

Josephine was shocked by the tone of his voice, but Joseph continued. "Could you spare some change for me and my sister? We have eaten little food and are very hungry."

"Money? You want money? Do you understand how hard I work for the money I make? And you think I'm going to give it to some poor beggar boy and his wretched sister? Listen to me boy, if I give you money, I'll have to give everyone money. Keep a close eye on the streets and you're bound to find a coin or two that someone has dropped along the way. Now move out of my sight. I have business to attend to."

He quickly flew past her and her brother almost knocking her down in the process. He hurried off not giving either one of them another thought and continued towards his destination.

Joseph turned to her. "Are you hurt?" Seeing that she was alright he stated, "I suppose father was right, we've been out here for over six hours and everyone is as bad as the last. Even our old family friend, Lord Henry..."

"I thought at least...," Josephine began. But she quickly cleared her throat and stood up tall, "No I refuse to give up. We've come too far. Come, Joseph, we must hurry it will be dark soon."

They walked another two miles with no success. Some pretended not see them and rushed past without a word, still, others spoke harshly to them, accusing them of trying to encroach upon their territory and demanded that they leave that part of the city, but others looked as poor as the royal pair pretended to be.

Joseph sighed aloud as they hit a dirt road that appeared to go on for miles, "Josephine we need to turn around now. We still have to walk all the way back to the castle before dinner is served, or mother will—"

"One more person Joseph, please. Look there's a house up ahead. We'll go up there and then turn around, I promise."

Joseph looked at his sister. She looked bedraggled and weary, but determined. "Alright."

They continued walking until they reached a small log cabin house. There was a horse and two mules in a stable on the right side of the house and in the back yard was a chicken coop with several chickens and a rooster. Josephine noticed a vegetable garden with several ripe vegetables and a nearby pig sty containing three very large pigs. In the distance, Joseph and Josephine saw a field with several cows and a few sheep grazing on a beautiful carpet of green grass. In the middle of the field, they saw a black dog sitting beside a young girl and an older man who were in the process of shearing sheep.

Joseph and Josephine slowly approached the fence that surrounded the land around the small log cabin house.

"Excuse me!" Josephine said loudly across the field to get the attention of the young girl.

The young girl looked up from the sheep that she was helping to shear and glanced towards Josephine.

"Can you help us, please," Josephine implored.

The young girl stood up from the stool where she sat and spoke to the older man kneeling beside her. The man looked towards the brother and sister, spoke briefly to the young girl and continued to shear the sheep. The young girl quickly walked over towards Josephine.

"Hello," the girl said.

"Hi," Josephine said returning her warm smile, "Would you be so kind to spare some milk from one of your cows for me and my brother? We have had very little food today and are very thirsty."

"And hungry!" Joseph spoke up standing a few feet away from the fence for fear that the young girl would hesitate to approach.

The girl looked towards Joseph and smiled, "Of course. We are always willing to share with all who are thirsty and hungry. Please wait here."

The young girl ran back to the older man and spoke quickly to him. She beckoned towards the pair several times as the old man continued to shear the sheep. The old man appeared not to be listening but then nodded his head in agreement.

The young girl returned and asked, "How much would you like?"

"A cup would be fine, my brother and I can share."

The girl nodded politely before heading off towards the log cabin. After a few minutes, she returned with two large hand carved wooden goblets filled to the rim with milk and a large loaf of bread tucked under her arm. She walked slowly towards Josephine.

"There is no need to share with your brother when we have

enough milk for you both," the girl said with a smile. "I have also provided bread for you both, but it is mostly for your hungry brother."

"Thank you." Josephine almost started to bow, but immediately remembered herself. "You are far too kind. What is your name?" Josephine asked gratefully.

"Katherine."

"Thank you, Katherine. I am grateful for the kindness you have shown me and my brother. My name is Josephine and he is Joseph."

"It was a pleasure to share what we have with you and your brother. Please enjoy your milk and bread and feel free to take the goblets with you."

"Do you not need them back?"

"If you should happen to pass this way again, you may return them. But if not, they are yours to keep."

"Thank you," Josephine said and curtsied.

Katherine curtsied in return, gave a soft wave to Joseph who continued to stand a few feet away and walked back to the field. When she reached the old man and the sheep, she turned and watched the strangers until they disappeared around the bend in the road.

The Young Woman

"What was the verdict on your first day out in the city?" King Jeremiah asked his daughter as he set down to eat the evening meal.

"For a while, it was exactly as you had said, father. No one wanted to help us at all. Not even your friend Lord Henry."

"Henry? Really?" Queen Gabriella said aloud, "I am surprised to hear that, he always seems like he would be the most generous out of our friends. All those stories he tells us during his visits…well, I suppose they must be only for show."

"Yes, but then we found a girl and she…" Joseph interrupted. "Well, you tell them, Josephine," Joseph said as excitement filled his voice.

"This girl was with an old man in the middle of a field shearing a sheep. They lived in a log cabin house and had cows, sheep, horses, and chickens. I came up to her and asked for a cup of milk for Joseph and me. She gladly obliged and brought me back two full glasses along with a loaf of bread, and then allowed us to keep the carved wooden goblets if we so chose."

Josephine and Joseph both held up their goblets as the story came to an end. Joseph watched as his mother smiled and as his father seemed to have a sparkle of hope in his eye.

"One person out of the thousands in my kingdom?" the king asked, "That's hard to believe."

"You said you would spare the kingdom for one person, am I not correct father?" Josephine asked searching her father's face for acknowledgement.

"Indeed you are. Why don't you and your brother go to the east end of the city tomorrow and see what you find over there, but be sure to pay a visit to this young woman again. See if she will not treat you with kindness and respect two days in a row. Do not take the goblets with you just yet. See how she reacts to you coming to visit her without bringing back her goblets that she lent to you," the king said as he began to stroke his graying beard.

"What are you thinking my darling?" the queen asked putting down her fork and taking a long hard look at her husband.

"I am trying to decide what I can do if this young girl indeed turns out to be a righteous person." He turned towards his children, "How old do you suppose she was?"

"She looked about Joseph's age father," Josephine spoke up.

"You don't say…now that does give me an idea."

The Challenge – Day Two

The next day Joseph and Josephine went to the East side of the kingdom and soon found out that it was no different than the North side. Joseph approached several noblemen and asked for help and received none. At one-point Joseph decided to go to a shop keeper's stand and ask for a few apples, but was thrown out into the street and was almost trampled by a team of horses that passed by carrying several noblemen. Josephine was frightened and angered by this and was close to losing hope just as her father had done. She decided that people were indeed selfish in their ways and that the entire city was corrupt, but then she remembered Katherine and decided it was time to pay her a visit.

Katherine was sitting outside the house churning butter and concentrating on pushing the plunger down and pulling it back up again. She didn't seem to notice them as they approached. The black dog from the day before was lying beside her and raised its head to give a small whine as Joseph and Josephine approached.

"There…there girl, what's got you?" she asked looking down at the dog and then into the distance where the king's children stood. She got up from her stool and ran to greet her visitors.

"Well hello again. What brings you by?" Katherine smiled at Josephine and then at Joseph who was standing a few feet away. "Why does your brother stand so far away? Would he not like to engage in our conversation as well?"

Josephine turned towards her brother and waved him over. "Hello," Joseph greeted Katherine as he approached. "I hope that you are not frightened by my presence."

Katherine smiled. "Not as long as you are not frightened by mine," she said as they both began to laugh.

A frown suddenly appeared on her face as she studied Joseph closely. She was silent for a time before she mumbled, "I'll be right back. Don't move."

Josephine and Joseph did as they were told. But Josephine quickly turned towards her brother and curiously eyed him as Katherine ran inside the small log cabin house. "Do you think she recognized you?"

"I suppose it's possible. You don't think she went inside to get a rope because she wants to hold us as hostages do you?"

"No, I doubt that," Josephine stated, but took two steps back away from the fence.

After several minutes passed, Katherine returned with another two wooden goblets in her hands filled to the brim once again with milk and a small sack of bread, butter and cheese under her left arm.

"Please take these and enjoy," Katherine said giving the goblets to Josephine and the sack of bread, butter, and cheese to Joseph.

"You look quite famished," she said over to Joseph. "I hope this will be enough for you. If you desire more, please let me know and I will do all I can to help."

"Thank you," Joseph said. "You have taken all this trouble for us. What can we do for you?"

"It's no trouble at all. What good is it to have extra food in your home if you cannot share it with friends?" Katherine asked. "Please take it. My family and I are more than happy to share."

"If you insist," Joseph said giving her a warm smile. "Thank you."

"It is our desire to help as we are able to do so," she said. She began to return to her butter churning, but turned around to say, "Please, you are welcome to come back and visit whenever you choose."

As Joseph and Josephine walked back, they spoke of the kindness of Katherine and wondered how their father would react upon hearing about their adventure. Joseph asked Josephine not to mention the incident with the horses earlier that day for fear that the king would be enraged. She promised not to do so but told Joseph that she understood her father's anger.

"Are you not surprised about the behavior of the people?" Josephine asked.

"Yes," Joseph said, "I am surprised and saddened. I did not think that it was as bad as father said. Now I see that he had good reason to be angry, but I am also thankful that we have found Katherine."

"I too and thankful. For we have found her to be both generous and kind."

The Kindness of a Stranger

"How was the East side of the village today children?" Queen Gabriella asked as she met her family around the table for the evening meal.

"Sadly…the same as the North side," Joseph answered.

"Were the people there as bad as the others? Did I not tell you so? I am disappointed as a King to be the ruler of these people."

"Yes, father. We do understand why you are angry. But we also followed your command and visited Katherine again today," Josephine said.

"Was it a fruitful visit?" Queen Gabriella asked as she used her fork to pierce one of the roasted potatoes on her plate.

"It was. We have found her to be generous, kind, and thoughtful. She never questioned us about yesterday's goblets, but instead gave us two more, although we never asked anything from her. I barely had the chance to mutter one word," Josephine said. She and Joseph held up their goblets as they had the day before. "She perceived that Joseph was hungry and therefore gave us a small sack of bread, butter, and cheese. We have not seen such kindness from one person in all of your kingdom."

"This is most certainly not what I had expected to hear from you after everything I saw during my one week beyond these castle walls. Although I can assure you that my heart is joyful that you have found this young woman," the King said before taking a drink from his silver goblet.

"So you will save this kingdom? Won't you father?"

"My word has gone out. I will not take it back. I will do as I have said. Tomorrow is your last day to go out into the city. Why don't you visit the South side? They have been known in the past for their hospitality and generosity, although when I passed through no one showed me any kindness. Perhaps they will show kindness to a brother and sister in need. Before you return home go and visit this young girl again. See if she will not treat you with kindness and generosity three days in a row, but you must do two things. You must return all four goblets. It was kind of her to lend them to you, but now you must return them to their rightful owner. Next, I want you to ask her a very specific question. She may deny you and call you greedy, but this is a question you must ask. Let me know where her gift comes from and her reaction to your question upon your return.

"What is the question we must ask father?" Joseph inquired.

The Challenge – Day Three

The next day Joseph and Josephine went to the South side of the kingdom but soon realized that it was no different from that of the North or East side. It was not as crowded in this part of the city. They recognized several noblemen and noblewomen about, but none that were willing to help poor beggar children. They were at the point of giving up when they saw another family friend.

"Should we approach her and ask for money or food?" Josephine asked. "I am sure that she would help. She is a dear friend of our mothers."

Joseph looked skeptical, "What more harm could befall to us now than has been already?"

They slowly approached their mother's friend, Eliza. She had visited them often at the castle and in their youth they frequently enjoyed the companionship of her two daughters. She doted on their mother and constantly spoke of how she always helped those that were "less fortunate."

"It is our duty you know to help those that are among the common sort," she could be heard saying as she dined with their mother.

"Excuse me miss," Josephine said approaching her. "Can you spare some change for my brother and me? We have been walking the streets of the city all day and are very hungry and thirsty."

She looked Josephine up and down. "How old are you my dear child?"

"Fourteen," Josephine replied. "But I will be fifteen soon."

"And where is your mother?" Eliza asked "Probably a woman of the streets, leaving her children on every street corner," she muttered.

"Sorry miss," Joseph answered. "We just want a little food."

"How sad. Do you know what's even sadder than that?" she asked as Josephine and Joseph shared a look of confusion before shaking their heads, "Heading over to your mother-in-law's house who is half dead with pneumonia and having two little beggars stop you on your way to your destination. Here", she said handing them one small bronze coin, "don't you ever bother me again and you better hope that she is still alive when I get there."

Their eyes followed her in wonder and fear as she walked away from them. "But she was always so nice," Josephine mumbled, "I must agree with father. Where are all the good citizens? Where are the people that treat each other with love, respect, and tenderness, instead of acting like we are a burden upon them? Is there no one righteous in this village?"

As they walked on Josephine passed by a beggar child holding a cup. She placed the bronze coin inside that she received from Eliza.

"Thank you, miss. God bless you miss!" he said smiling.

"There is one person." Joseph declared as they walked passed the beggar child who was now staring in awe at the bronze coin, "Come. Let us see if we can intrude upon her kindness one more time before she throws us out like everyone else has."

"Let us hope that, this is not the case," Josephine frowned following in the footsteps of her brother.

• • •

Katherine was waiting outside the gate of her small log cabin home when they approached. She watched as they slowed down in their tracks and glanced cautiously towards one another before continuing towards her.

"I was hoping the two of you would stop by again today. I have quite begun to look forward to your visits and you always seem to stop by around this time."

"You were hoping we would stop by today?" Joseph asked quizzically.

"Yes, please. I have something I would like to show you, but you must wash up first." She led them around the side of the house to a large black water pump and a large metal bucket.

"Wash first and I will meet you inside," Katherine stated. She laid a small yellow towel beside the bucket and walked back to the front of the house.

"What do you think this means?" Joseph asked washing his

hands and face slightly.

"Do you think she wants us to meet someone, but has to make sure that we are presentable?" Josephine asked as she began to wash her hands and arms.

Joseph looked down at himself and laughed. "Do I look presentable to you?"

Josephine shook her head as she chuckled at her brother and finished washing her face. After they had both finished she and her brother walked back to the front of the house.

"Come in. Don't worry. You are among friends here," Katherine laughed as she beckoned them inside. They followed her inside the small house only to find a table occupied by four men and seven places marked by plates filled with food. "Let me introduce you to my brothers. This is Thomas, Simon, and Ronald. And this is my father Phineas."

"Please to meet you," Josephine and Joseph said in unison.

As they looked around the table Josephine leaned in to whisper into Joseph's ear, "That is the older man that we saw out in the field the first day with Katherine." Joseph looked at the man that his sister was talking about and nodded in agreement.

"I hope you don't mind, but I asked my father if I could invite the two of you in for dinner. I thought that this would be better than bringing food out to you and letting you go on your way to eat and walk. It is good to sit down together with friends to a decent meal and good conversation."

"This is too much. I don't know what to say," Josephine muttered.

"I assure you that it's not that much at all. But we did what we could, with what we had," Katherine continued to talk as she watched Joseph make himself at home. He introduced himself to her brothers and father and took a seat to the right of Thomas, who was the eldest. "It looks as though your brother has already made himself quite comfortable. Come let us join them," she said taking Josephine's hand in hers. She placed Josephine to the left of her so that she was in the middle of her two visitors.

"Oh!" Josephine said aloud suddenly remembering the bag

she brought with her, "We have returned your goblets that you have generously allowed us to borrow."

"Thank you for returning my goblets," the dad said with a chuckle, "now we can add them to the others." Josephine watched as Phineas gestured to the open kitchen cabinet filled with dozens of wooden goblets that closely resembled the ones that she was returning. "I work with wood a lot and this is one of the many hobbies that I have picked up on over the years. Although it would not have mattered if you would have returned them or not. I can always make more. Nonetheless, I am thankful that Katherine could share some of our belongings with you, I have raised my children in the way of the Lord, hoping that they always remember that they should treat others in the way they would want to be treated."

"Katherine certainly has a way of doing that," Joseph stated.

"Then my job is done."

"Shall we pray?" Katherine asked as she looked around the table.

"I will pray," her brother Simon said, "Dear Lord, thank you for this day that you have gratefully bestowed upon us. Thank you for allowing us to show kindness to our visitors today and all the strangers around us in the city. Thank you for allowing us to humble ourselves and bring glory to your name. Please bless this meal that has been placed before us and bless the hands that have prepared it. Amen."

"Amen," everyone around the table said in unison.

Soon everyone had begun to eat the food that had been placed in front of them. Katherine and her family did not have much, but they had enough to feed themselves and a few visitors. Thomas had killed a chicken and prepared it, while Simon, the middle brother, had milked the cows and drawn water from the well for them to drink. Katherine and Ronald worked together to pick vegetables from the garden in the back of the house and worked in the kitchen for a few hours so that their guests would have some soup. Phineas had also pitched in as much as he could, by making some small biscuits from the flour they had, once he returned home from work. He had smiled seeing his children all pitch in around the house to try and prepare supper for the night. Over the years, this sight was one that always made him smile.

"Joseph, Josephine…we have a tradition in this house that while we are sitting down to dinner we tell one another either, something that we are thankful for or what we have learned today. We would be honored as a family if you would join in on our tradition."

They both nodded in response as Thomas began to speak, "I am thankful for my family and the food that has been prepared before us today."

"We can all see that you are thankful for food," Katherine laughed, "your plate is already empty."

"And with that…I am also very thankful for seconds," Thomas said as he reached for the large wooden bowl of remaining soup.

Everyone around the table chuckled as Simon cleared his throat and began, "Today I learned that we should not take life for granted. I have been blessed with a family, food, clothing, and a roof over my head, but there are many people in the world who do not have what I do."

"Thank you for sharing that with us Simon," Phineas spoke up, "Did you see something today in the village that made you come to that conclusion?"

"There was an entire family living on the streets. A father, mother, and their three children, sitting outside a clothing store as their own clothes had been ripped to shreds from weeks of wear and tear. They were bone thin and looked as if they had not eaten for days. I bought them each a loaf of bread, but I continue to wonder, what will happen to them tomorrow…or maybe a week or a month into the future. If they last that long…I wish there was something we could do."

"Maybe we should talk to the king!" Thomas spoke up in-between bites of his food, "Perhaps if he knew the life style and the suffering of some of his citizens he could help."

"Perhaps. But that family is one in a million. You have no idea how many people passed them by and never tried to help them or offer their services. But I suppose that is what our world is being reduced to. People only care about themselves."

"That is the exact reason why God destroyed the city of Sodom and Gomorrah. We have become a selfish being, only caring about ourselves and what we can gain, that we have forgotten all about our neighbors," Katherine said solemnly, "sometimes I wish that we had the power to change things. I don't want to end up like that city."

Joseph and Josephine gazed knowingly at one another before Phineas interrupted. "Joseph, what is it that you are thankful for or what is something that you have learned today?"

"I am thankful that I was invited in to dinner with your lovely family. Not only that, but my eyes have been opened in a way tonight, that you will never truly understand."

• • •

After dinner, Joseph and Josephine offered their hands to help Katherine's family wash the dishes and put away what was left of the dinner. Katherine watched in silence as Joseph gave scrap after scrap of food to her dog, Porridge. Once or twice Joseph turned his attention from Porridge and looked up and met her gaze. They both smiled in response, but Katherine quickly turned from him and brought her attention back to that of Josephine and her brothers as they finished up with the dishes.

"We wanted to thank you for inviting us to dinner," Josephine said as she began to head towards the door with Joseph. "It meant more to us than words could ever describe."

"It is no problem. Perhaps you can join us again for dinner one day soon," Katherine said as she looked over at her father.

"I have no problem with the idea. You two are welcome to join us whenever you like."

"Thank you," Joseph and Josephine said in unison.

"Well, we better get going. Mother is probably ready to send the royal guard after us," Joseph said jokingly.

Josephine looked over at her brother and gave him a look of apprehension, but no one else seemed to find anything odd about his comment.

"Father," Katherine began, "Can't we allow Thomas to drive them home in the wagon? It is late out and they will have a long walk back."

"No thank you," Josephine quickly spoke up, "we couldn't think to bother you with a ride home."

"It is no problem at all," Phineas said. "I can have Thomas to get the wagon ready as soon as he finishes putting away the last of the dishes."

"No sir." Joseph spoke up, "As kind of a gesture as that is, we couldn't impose upon you any more than we already have. We will be fine by ourselves. We are familiar with the long walk home by now."

"Nonsense," Thomas said as he turned away from the dish pan and began to dry his hands on a small white towel, "it will only take me a moment."

Joseph looked towards Josephine as she nudged him in the side to try and convince Katherine's family otherwise. Phineas watched the siblings closely and picked up on the tension that was beginning to grow between them.

"If you prefer to walk back home alone, I will leave that decision up to you," Phineas said, "but know that the offer will always stand."

Joseph looked towards Phineas as a wave of relief passed in front of his eyes, "Thank you sir...for all of your kindness and generosity. We must be going now, but we will remember to come back and visit you when we can."

"We will see you all soon," Josephine said as she followed her brother through the front door.

Katherine's family waved the siblings down the road until they could no longer see them.

"Father, why did you not allow for Thomas to take them home at this late hour?" Katherine asked.

"I could see it in their eyes that they did not want to be a burden upon us. Plus, the way that they were eying one another... they may be ashamed of where they live and did not want us to see it."

Saving the Kingdom

King Jeremiah and Queen Gabriella were waiting outside when their children returned. Upon seeing them the Queen immediately raced towards them and brought them in for a big hug. "We were beginning to worry. It has been two hours passed the time you were supposed to have returned home. What happened? Is everything okay?"

"Yes mother, everything is fine," Joseph said looking in the direction of his father. "Father we need to speak with you."

"About what my child? Did the young girl not give you what I asked you to ask her? Was it too much of a request to borrow a horse?"

"Honestly father," Josephine spoke up with her head lowered, "we forgot to ask her. Our minds and hearts were otherwise occupied."

Queen Gabriella looked at her sorrowful children's faces, "Let us not stay outside at this hour. Come in…you must be starving." Once everyone had gathered around the dining room table the king and queen watched as their children slowly picked at the food in front of them. "Are neither of you hungry this evening?"

"Does it have something to do with what you wanted to tell us? Or why you were late this evening?" the king asked.

"Katherine is not the only righteous person in the kingdom," Joseph said as he allowed his fork to fall onto his plate.

"You have found others?" The king's face lit up as he began to wonder where the others might be located.

"Sort of…they happen to be the rest of Katherine's family."

Joseph and Josephine quickly went into the details of what had happened only hours before at dinner with Katherine's family.

"Well, I suppose that explains why she is the way she is," the queen said thoughtfully, "she was raised well by her father. As were her brothers."

"They shall all be rewarded," the king said to no one in particular. "But Katherine more than the others. For if it were not for her we would have lost hope, destroyed the kingdom, and never found her family."

Josephine nodded in reply to her father's words, "What have you decided to bestow upon her father?"

"A husband."

All heads turned to look at Joseph.

His mouth was agape while his eyes were stretched open wide. "What?

"I have decided that this is the best gift to bestow upon this young woman. To be married into the royal family...and as the royal family it is our responsibility to be the example for this kingdom. Having Katherine, the one righteous person that you found, joining this family through marriage is exactly what my kingdom needs," the king replied easily.

"But...I don't even know her."

"You will have time once you are wed to get to know one another."

Joseph opened his mouth to speak but was quickly cut off by his sister. "Father as nice of a gesture as that is. I do believe that Katherine will have the same response as my brother. They do not know one another. It has only been three days and only for a few minutes each time."

"Your mother and I never had the privilege of meeting, not once before our wedding day. Why should his wedding be any different?" the king responded with a firm tone.

"Perhaps," Queen Gabriella began, placing a hand on her husband's shoulder. "We can come up with a compromise that works for both parties. Suppose we allow Katherine and Joseph to court for a time to get to know one another. Then afterwards they can be free to marry...if that is their united decision."

The king solemnly looked from his wife to Joseph, "I suppose I will allow this to be your decision, my son."

Joseph nodded gratefully towards his father and mother as he closed his eyes and whispered a prayer that was hidden from the ears of his family. As he finished he opened his eyes and looked towards his father, "I will do as you ask, as long as we have the opportunity to court for a time."

The king bowed his head in response to his son's request, "I will do as you ask of me."

"Thank you, father."

"Lucas!" the king bellowed as he walked over to pull a long red and gold cord that hang from the ceiling at the far end of the room.

"Yes m'lord," Lucas said as he bowed low before the royalty in the room.

"Find Stephan and prepare two carriages at dawn tomorrow morning. I have a task for you both."

Meeting the One

The King took a moment to look the girl, her brothers, and
her father up and down as they entered the throne room. The
family was a darker color than that of his own family, he noticed.
The girl and her brothers had dark black hair that resembled
the color of charcoal, while the father's hair had already started
turning a light shade of silver. Katherine was short in stature but
walked tall in confidence not knowing what lied ahead for her.

She stood tall as she took her place before the king with
her father and brothers at her right hand side. They all bowed to
honor him and waited for him to speak.

"Please do not bow to me, it is I who should be bowing
to you, Katherine," The king said as he rose from his chair,
descended the throne, and bowed low before her, "and your
lovely family."

"Why should you bow before me, my Lord? What have I…
we…done to deserve such an unspeakable honor?"

"You have chosen righteousness over selfishness," the king
said walking back to his throne. "Although you did not know that
my son and daughter were the children of a king, you still treated
them with kindness, respect, and the honor that they deserved.
That is what makes a righteous person. Being selfless above all
else."

"Your daughter and son, my Lord?"

As the words exited her mouth the doors to the throne room
opened and Josephine entered the room with Joseph falling into
step beside her.

"Those are the guests we had over for dinner last night,"
Simon said in a hushed whisper.

"Well I suppose we know now why they didn't want me to
drive them home," Thomas replied.

Katherine stared at her friends for a time before turning her
attention back to the King, "But my Lord, I have done nothing
that no other person would not do themselves."

"That is just it. No one else did what you did. Not one.

Besides your family of course," the King shook his head in defeat.

Katherine remained silent but looked up at her father with grief in her eyes. He looked back at her with a smile that brought tears to her face. Katherine turned from him and looked towards the floor.

"You and your family do not come from much, but you were willing to share everything you had with two complete strangers. That is more than I can say for the richest man living in my kingdom. He wants to keep his Earthly riches to himself and refuses to share with those less fortunate than him. With that being said—"

As he spoke the queen entered the throne room and passed by her children. Katherine and her family turned around to look at her as she entered. As she approached them they all bowed low to grace her presence. "Rise dear. There is no need to bow…any of you," the queen looked over at Katherine's father and brothers and nodded for them to rise as well. "We asked you to come because we wanted to thank you."

"Thank me? For what your majesty?"

"For saving the kingdom, that's what," Josephine spoke up from where she stood at the back of the room.

"I don't understand…" Katherine said.

"That is not of importance at this time. What is important is what I can do for you for being the only righteous person in my entire kingdom," the king said, his voice booming over the room. "I would like to offer you the hand of my son Joseph in marriage."

"What?" Katherine said.

"It is as I said. I tried to think of countless rewards I could offer you, but this was my final decision. To have you become a part of my family and for our two families to be joined together as one. I would not want my son to marry anyone else in the kingdom as long as you are alive and walk on this Earth."

"Marriage?"

Katherine looked over at Joseph for an answer. He stood and looked back at her with a warmth and tenderness in his eyes that she couldn't quite understand. She like Joseph well enough, but she had always thought it would be a few more years before she was married. And now she was to be married to a prince? Going from peasant to princess in a matter of seconds was a lot to consume.

"Of course a long courtship will be first so that you can better know one another. That was Joseph's only one stipulation," Queen Gabriella stated.

"I can help you with planning your wedding when the time comes and with your training to become a princess," Josephine said.

"Your family is also welcome to stay here if they wish. We have already arranged a living space and room for each member of your family. What I really want to say, Katherine," the King said as he descended from his throne and took her by the hand, "is thank you. Thank you for being generous and outgoing when it could have been just as easy to turn away from my children. Thank you, for treating your neighbors with kindness, respect, and in the way that you would like to be treated. Thank you for being the hope that I needed to see, for being faithful to your heavenly father when you could have easily turned away. But overall, thank you for being the one righteous person that saved my kingdom from being destroyed. So Katherine, what do you say to my offer?"

A Dream Interrupted

Look into my eyes and tell me you love me.
Watch the sunset with me again and say you don't need me.
Hold me close and say that you don't want me.
Kiss me.

How did everything get to this point?
What can I do to erase time and go back to the moment,
where everything made sense?

Stare into my eyes like I'm the only person alive.
Interrupt my dreams and I'll never be awoken again.
Let's watch the stars together once more.
Kiss me.

Wipe my tears as I long for the past.
Pray with me as I ask for a future with you.
Laugh with me about past memories.
Hug me for the last time and never let me go.

Tell me how you wish things could be different.
Talk to me about the future you had dreamed up for us.
Whisk me away to a place where nothing can separate us.
Kiss me.

Let me tell you how much you mean to me.
Allow me to finally say that *I love you*.

This Happened at My Church

"Raise your hand if you have ever felt intimidated by an African American?"
All hands raised. Really?
Not everyone feels this way. I tried to convince myself of that as I looked around the room.
My once assumed friends approached the set up microphones in the middle of the isles.
Our turn will be next. Our voices will be heard.
"Why are they so loud?"
"Why are they so demanding and pushy?"
"Why do they try so hard to be like us?"
"Do they actually remember what their real hair looks like?"
Questions came and went.
We weren't allowed to answer.
I could no longer look up to see who spoke at the microphones.
Soon everyone was dismissed. They quickly exited through the double doors. They laughed and talked like nothing had happened. As if nothing had changed.
We never got a turn to speak. It wasn't for us. It was for them.

I'll Wait

The clock strikes twelve,
but, there is no golden carriage turning
into an orange pumpkin,
I see no horses transforming into tiny mice,
and there is no prince charming chasing
after me with a glass slipper.
So I'll wait.

I see a carpet,
it doesn't fly and take me to far off places
around the world,
there is no genie in a lamp ready
to grant all of my wishes,
and there is no man willing to risk
his life for me.
So I'll wait.

I am asleep,
It's not as long a sleep as you'd think,
I'm not pleased to be in a tower guarded
by a fire-breathing dragon,
there's no witch smiling
because she thinks I'm dead,
and there is no prince attempting to fight the beast
so that he may kiss and wake me up.
So I'll wait.

There is a frog,
when I kiss it, it doesn't turn into a prince or I a frog, we do not go
off on an adventure in the deep depths of the forest,
we do not fall in love nor are we restored
to humans by a single kiss.
No, because it's just a frog, and I'm just a girl.
So I'll wait.

however

There is a prince,
Who searched for me and found me,
he fought the dragon for me,
he woke me up out of a long death-sleep

when he whispered my name,
he loves me unconditionally,
he loves me for me, despite all of my flaws.
He calls me to him and is ready to marry me
and spend the rest of eternity with me.
I am his princess, his bride.

This prince died for me and was resurrected
from his tomb,
he knows my every need and desire without
a single hint from me.
He is faithful to the very end of time,
so please hear me when I say that my prince
is greater than all of these other princes.
So I'll wait, yes, I will wait on you, Jesus,
my darling prince charming.

Waiting for the Concert to Begin

The room was full of impatient fans.
The hoodie she wore made her ten times hotter.

The red solo cups, were filled with beer,
that let out a scent that soon filled the air.

She regretted not buying a seat as her back began to ache.
A girl behind her began to complain about the wedges that hugged
her feet.

She wished silently that she was small enough to sit on her
brother's shoulders, if only to see over the heads of the taller boys
that blocked her view.

A boy in front of her looked at his watch and told his friend that
he wouldn't be staying long.
"Chill. It's not like you have anywhere better to be," his friend said.

A girl beside her kept tossing her long blonde hair in her face. She
silently began to wish for a pair of scissors.

The audience was beginning to grow restless.
Some began to chant, *Tori, Tori.*

Someone behind her spilled their beer. It silently splashed against
her right leg and found a spot inside her shoe.

"Dangit" they said, "Better get another refill."
It was time to go, it was time –

The room grew dark and the fans began to cheer wildly.
Everything that she had felt. That they had felt. Immediately
disappeared.

Acknowledgments

I would like to thank my Father, Rochaun Hawkins, for his unfailing support and words of encouragement; my Mother, Diane Hawkins, for her awesome time, effort, editing skills, helpful criticism, and the ideas that helped to make all of these short stories possible; my brother, Samuel Hawkins, for his awesome ideas (no matter how outlandish they were); and my sister and brother-in-law, Shekirah and Lloyd Looper, for proofreading my stories in their spare time and their ideas that helped inspire a few of my poems. My dear friends Todd McDonald, and Becca Slaback for proofreading my stories for me and helping them to be the best that they can be. Also I would like to thank my sister once again for inspiring the story behind *Faith Like a Mustard Seed.*

Most of all I wish to thank my Father in Heaven, because without him none of my past works, recent, or future works would be possible.